DIVERSE KNOTS

DIVERSE KNOTS

US Citizens

AWATEF A

Copyright © Awatef A.

All rights reserved. No part of this book may be reproduced in any form or by any electronic or mechanical means, including information storage and retrieval systems, without permission in writing from the publisher, except by reviewers, who may quote brief passages in a review.

ISBN: 978-1-63649-977-2 (Paperback Edition)
ISBN: 978-1-63649-978-9 (Hardcover Edition)
ISBN: 978-1-63649-976-5 (E-book Edition)

Some characters and events in this book are fictitious. Any similarity to real persons, living or dead, is coincidental and not intended by the author.

Book Ordering Information

Phone Number: 347-901-4929 or 347-901-4920
Email: info@globalsummithouse.com
Global Summit House
www.globalsummithouse.com

Printed in the United States of America

CONTENTS

Acknowledgments ix

Chapter 1: No More! 1
Chapter 2: Neighbors Indeed 7
Chapter 3: Killer Looks 15
Chapter 4: A Helping Handful 23
Chapter 5: Historic Drive-Through 27
Chapter 6: Best Feast! 31
Chapter 7: Airport Threat 35
Chapter 8: What Goes Up? 39
Chapter 9: Gunned Down 49
Chapter 10: Here Goes Nowhere! 63
Chapter 11: Kidnapped 67
Chapter 12: The Park 77
Chapter 13: Hospital Return 85
Chapter 14: Home Sweet Home? 93
Chapter 15: Traditional Court 99
Chapter 16: Out of Sight 103
Chapter 17: Judicial Love 109
Chapter 18: Washed Away! 129
Chapter 19: Knot Twist! 135

Let there be peace on earth,
and may it begin at my hands.
Unconditional conditions are sometimes conditioned to
conditionally exist.

ACKNOWLEDGMENTS

Hope is the greatest weapon for survival and victory.

CHAPTER ONE

No More!

I flew around in my bedroom like a bird with a broken wing. My determined mind wouldn't rest until my quest for freedom had been achieved. I decided to leave that prison-home not one second later. Despite my overwhelming fear of getting caught, I could not stand that man and place any longer. I managed to gather my thoughts and my strength to prepare for my risky escape. Trapped in a double domestic war zone, I knew I could defeat the impossible and make it out of that land. Dead or alive in the attempt, I owed it to myself to be saved. The need for survival served me well in a desperate situation; heroes were rare, and therefore, I had to find the hero within. Palestine shared a cold and violent war against Israel. One land shaped like a stretched rubber pie by two opposing forces. Why didn't anyone refer to it as a civil war or as a domestic war? The country stood as one despite their denials of each other's existence. My opinion differed from the rest: I believed that we shared a one God, a mother, and a father; Adam and Eve. We believed in heaven and acknowledge the existence of hell. We have faith that there is a Judgment Day in the Hereafter. Peace required effort from both sides, and all it war just one to start. I wished to solve the Middle East crisis ever since I opened my eyes to its soil, trees, clear skies, and the different animals that roamed around like pedestrians. It remained my priority and greatest fantasy to make the two nations settle down in accepted manners. How one human being could torture or kill another and be able to live with her/himself. The dusted years of quarrelling made people overlook the obvious. Lack of knowledge and patience made the two nations split and attach, all at the same time. I witnessed disorder despite the ruthless rules set aside. Conflicts branched out to the rest of the world, yet it handicapped politicians from finding a resolution. I faced abuse and domestic discomfort from inside and outside. I communicated to the Israeli soldiers in the English language in necessary situations. My husband and I went to review his immigration papers that I'd filed for him. Being married to an American citizen granted him the privilege of a chance at obtaining American residency.

Sammy, my dreaded husband, had little, if no education, even in the Arabic language. It drove him mad when I spoke English, especially to the Israeli clerks at the immigration office in Jerusalem. He became convinced that I shared a ridiculous flirt with the Israeli man. He threatened me all the way home and aimed at exposing me in a slanderous notion. The big crime occurred when the Israeli clerk smiled as he handed me my passport back. If only my husband had understood what the soldier said, he may have fought him and ended up in jail. The Israeli soldier said, "What's a beautiful woman like you doing with that?" He implied my husband. I did my best to maintain a blank face. Sammy instantly became threatened with jealousy and rage. Anyone could see the difference between Sammy and I from a mile away. His harsh and loud voice diminished my natural low-toned speech. He screamed for attention and always received it by fighting with someone or something. His overweight and tall bone structure made him appear muscular. He had a beard to make up for the bald shave of his head. He waited until we stepped into the house and struck me as hard as he could on my face. He pulled my hair and wiped the floor with my face. "That face of yours is not so pretty now." I couldn't understand how he showed no remorse or feelings of shame for his destructive beatings. He pushed, shoved, and slapped me around. He gave up once he noticed I had lost all my resistance and became completely helpless. He finished with victory on his behalf. He took a break and headed to celebrate with his friends. Once he left, I stood up with rage and anger. "That's it, that's the last time!" I didn't know if I meant that phrase for me or for Sammy. I took one last look in the mirror to put my disorganized hair together. I became blinded by the flow of tears in my eyes. I hated feeling sorry for myself, but that time, I never looked more pitiful. I cried like an out-of-control baby. I had no time to waste; I needed to leave before my so-called husband returned. There were many knots in my long black hair; I had no time to untangle. Most often, he went for my hair when he first started with me. Maybe if it was shorter, he would have hesitated. It was easier for me to blame my hair for getting pulled than to find a logical reason why he did it anyway. I was not allowed to cut it: it was one of his properties, and it came with the territory. I could not find the brush from the mess he created after the rumble. I just used my jittering fingers as a comb. I quickly strung a ponytail. Taking some action helped stop me from crying, but not completely. I wiped my face with my hands and ran around the merciless bedroom, searching for my most prized possession, my American passport. It was my only token for survival. "Where are you? Please be there!" It fell out of my purse when Sammy snatched my purse off my shoulder and tossed it across the bedroom. "Oh, thank God," I said as I noticed its dark blue color underneath the bed. I reached down and picked it up. I ran across the room to get my purse and thrust my passport in it. I opened my purse and mindlessly dropped whatever caught my eye into it. I thought to myself. I put on my flat and comfortable pair of shoes as I put on my favorite on-the-run black shirt. With my purse on my shoulder, I button my shirt. I realized I was off one button; I couldn't afford any time to fix it. Besides, my thumb and palm bled from the broken glass mirror. Sammy broke it when he threw his ashtray at it to give me a scare. A piece of glass flew across the room toward me; luckily, I put up my hands up in defense to protect my face. I threw on a long and rectangular head scarf on my head. I did not want to be easily recognized by the neighbors. They served as watchdogs for my tyrant husband. They all believed I deserved to be mistreated because they didn't help to put an end to his violent behavior. My mother-in-law filled the town with indecent rumors about me. She had a loud voice and spoke a lot, so if you were sitting with her, you had no choice but to hear and listen to what she had to say. "Salwa was ruined by the western culture, and we need to teach her our values in Palestine," she would demand. I feared that one day I would curse her out loud to her and her son.

"Is that a new rule to add to the list?" I said, without thinking for a moment of the consequences to follow. He pushed me to the wall. Without any control of balance, I hit the wall and fell to the floor. He watched me struggling to sit upward against the closet. You disgrace me when you refused to come back to this town and marry me. Now I have you, and I'm going to make you pay till the day you die. Tell me, who did you want instead, a rich American man? We were arranged for each other ever since we were kids. Your father did the right thing: he forced you to marry me." I had to hear that speech every time his anger sparked against me. For five years of endless torture, I had to bear his wrath. People wondered why we couldn't conceive any children. How could I with all that physical inflictions he put me through. His accusations of me having a past lover were more painful than the beating itself. If I had a lover, I would not have been captured in such a dreadful marriage. My father did a good job at hiding me. When he wasn't hiding me, he was spying on me by sending my two brothers, to dictate my every move. I fought hard and earned my high school diploma. College was never an option. Therefore, I attended college courses in high school and earned a few credits that made me feel good for a while. I lost the fight before I even started for higher education. Since my early teenage years, I was not permitted to attend any parties or large gatherings. They thought the less I saw, the more innocent I would remain. From a control freak father to an abusive spouse, I had endured. I resented my father more than anyone, even more than my husband. My father gave me away to his nephew without consulting with me. I had no say in the matter despite my unheard objections. I pleaded to my relatives to stop the marriage from taking place. They assumed I had my eyes set on someone else. They couldn't understand that I couldn't stand to marry my cousin, but I ended up marrying him anyway. His actions were justified by the community and accepted. Prison made him more of a man, they claimed; I viewed him as a beast. I received no support at twenty-five years of age. The women in my town were excessively jealous beings in nature. They shunned me off on any occasion. Just because I spent most of my life in America, I didn't fit in. To their standards, I had broken the first rule for fitting in and that being my attempt to reject my cousin's marriage proposal. I was viewed as a star, yet everyone tried to bring me down and defame me. I avoided every man in that town for fear of slander.

With luck on my side, he retrieved his abuse and walked away. "Get up and make me something to eat," he ordered. "Then I'll see what I'm going to do to you," he said sadistically. I remained seated until he left my sight. He walked away to the bathroom. Without any hesitation, I reached from under the bed for my purse and slid it from underneath. I stood up and ignored all the pain I encompassed. I ran to the door and wrestled with opening it despite my fractured thumb. I stormed out and made it past the gate. The sun was steaming and the ground felt like the moon, no gravity to pull me back into that house ever again. I felt as if I broke loose from hell. Going back to my family and father was the lesser of two hells. I left him burning in his own fury. I considered the war between him and me over from that moment on. When two parties didn't get along, separation served as a better option. I understood why the fighting among Palestinians and the Israelis lasted that long. They were both very opposite, yet refused to submit to one another, even in negotiated peace talks. They always followed a rupture of some sort, which hindered peace from ever occurring. Simplicity required a perfect plan. I wished to come up with that plan and change the living conditions in that land. First, I needed to help myself out of my own domestic and imperfect relationship. I had to start somewhere, and home destroyed my capabilities.

CHAPTER TWO

Neighbors Indeed

I didn't care for the neighbors or anyone anymore. I ran out of that town like a cheetah. Never did I ever feel such an adrenaline rush as I did, racing out of that ignorant place. I heard my husband Sammy call from a distance, "Salwa, Salwa!" I kept running without turning around. I skimmed through the streets, and everyone seemed invisible to my watery eyes. It wasn't long before I reached the security border that intersected the city of Ramallah. There were at least six Israeli soldiers scattered around at the checking point. I found myself running toward them. I looked behind me and noticed that Sammy had yielded. He was intimidated to get closer. I didn't mind getting in trouble with the Israeli authority. I knew I had a better chance with them than Sammy. They were not very accepting of my exasperated approach. I was stopped. One soldier held my right arm firmly. "Hey, hey, what are you doing?" a soldier said. He took a hard and scrutinizing look at my shattered face. I noticed he had more freckles than I did. "I am an American citizen and I need help," I said while digging inside my purse for my passport. Another soldier snatched my purse from my shaking hands. He carefully looked inside my purse and then held it in his hand. "We will take you to headquarters and have a chat over there," he mocked. I was held by two soldiers and was driven in an olive-colored army jeep. In the middle of all that trouble, I couldn't help but feel a pleasant breeze cooling my face. I looked over to the soldier on my left side and said, "Please look inside my purse and you will find my passport." He did not respond. It was obvious that a bigger authority needed to check into my provocative move of running to them the way I did. My eyes streamed over the rocky and bumpy land with pebbles and dust covering the territory. I saw the olive trees: they appeared old and sad. They've been around for centuries and knew too much. The fig trees that served as neighbors to the olive trees seemed dehydrated and tired as its branches hung low. If they could speak, they would complain about the lack of holiness the Holy Land had become. Respect seeds didn't make it there. War made everyone protective and possessive. I guessed that could have been one of the reasons Sammy treated me like property. It couldn't have been right. I thought if you love something, you take good care of it. Love faced the biggest oppression in the country. Each side claiming they love it when all they contributed was destruction. Some home they made it, full of bloodshed and disorder. Walking on that land felt like walking on needles. If I ran, I got hurt; if I stood, I still got pain. I decided to fly away as the best option. I used the ride with the two soldiers to regain some of my strength and energy back. The two soldiers looked at me with surprised eyebrows; I felt I had nothing to fear. I could teach them that I intended no harm by being calm and peaceful. I used to see Palestinians ride in similar vehicles, but with great resistance and struggle. I, on the other hand, sat willingly, and that made me look crazy. I had hoped to be treated with positive prejudice. American citizens were given better privileges than the

Palestinian citizens. Although I was a Palestinian woman, I felt confident in my case and remained optimistic. I knew I had the right evidence of my nonthreatening intentions. I was escorted into an old and gloomy building. Held by two soldiers on either side, I showed no resistance to being escorted inside the building. We walked up through the narrow hallway and entered one of the rooms. Fear started to take over my confidence and hopes. "You need to wait till I get the General to look at you," said the soldier with the freckles. They ordered me to take a seat in the large office with soldiers walking around like Wall Street. The office had a television on the upper corner of the room. They had it turned on the news in Hebrew. Soldiers passed by me and gave me questionable looks. I comforted myself. The soldiers walked away with my purse. I stood up from my chair, only to feel a big hand on my shoulder pushing me back down. I looked up and noticed a well-built soldier. "Where is my purse? I need my purse!" I called out loud. "We need to examine it first and then we'll get back to you," he said and walked away with his partner. They met with another group of soldiers and spoke Hebrew. I didn't speak that language, but I knew I was the subject spoken of. Paranoia had the best of me. I anxiously awaited my fate. I couldn't go anywhere, I thought to myself. The place felt like a gym: activity and restlessness conquered it. Three hours later, the two soldiers came to me and, without any explanation, held me by the arms. We walked to another private office. The sign on the door read "General David Weisman." Two men were in the room. The soldiers tucked me inside the room and left. They shut the door from behind me. With no more confidence, I felt frightened. One of the men was wearing a unique soldier's uniform; he was at least fifty years old, I assumed. He had more ornaments and badges that gave his uniform some color. He was husky and had a strange frown on his face. I could see the light reflect off his bald head. I feared looking in his eyes. He had my purse right in front of him. He seemed to have invaded it shamelessly. I practically forgot what I had trashed into it besides my passport. With a few personal items and little cash, I needed it anyway. "Come in, and have a seat," he said with a deep-toned voice. I looked at the adjacent seat by the other seated gentleman. He wore a blue navy-colored suit. Last time I saw a man dressed up in a sharp suit was when I came back from America. At the airport, I encountered and bumped into a man dressed in similar fashion. He disappeared all at once. He also seemed like a businessman of some sort, and he seemed in his blossoming thirties. In my town, the only time I saw a man in a suit was on his wedding day. Formal wear also came from those who recently arrived from America or any other outside country such as Brazil or Spain. I took the order quietly and sat on the chair that stood by the General's desk. I looked at the handsome man across from me. I became angry when I realized he helped in the intrusion of my belongings in my purse. I remembered I had my secretly written novel in it. He flipped the pages, reading a little bit from each page. In my spare and rarely free time, I wrote a bloody novel. A mirroring of Romeo and Juliet's story, the only difference was the lovers were a Palestinian Muslim female and an Israel Jewish man. I found it difficult to dictate a happy ending. I assumed I had to be happy in order to project it well. When I wrote a forbidden love story, I never imagined it could have been illegal. I dared to come up with an idea like that. I might have written it to spite my father, if it should one day get published. I aimed to keep it hidden from everyone until I get back to New York City. The best values and rules I learned growing up in the States. Diversity and tolerance were taught to my generation at public schools. That to me represented freedom by itself. Why couldn't people in the Holy Land live the same way? I disliked the way the man seated across from me skipped through the pages. I wanted to tell him that every page had meaning and depth. Who was I to have spoken? Silence is my biggest defense. With his face buried in the pages, he appeared drawn in. "Tell me, Ms. Adam, what is your story, or is it the one written over there?" he said, pointing to my novel in the gentleman's hands. "I know that you can help me travel back to the US," I said, pivoting my body toward his seated direction. "Just like that, you thought? Do you take us to a flying agency?" he asked. A slight chuckle leaked from the other man. "What are you running away from?" hurt me having to share my story with anyone; it hurt me more when they didn't help. I felt compelled to give the General a try. He seemed open for anything despite his stiffness. I felt my emotions getting the best of me. My voice stuttered. I dished my heart out and said the truth that I had not been able to mention to any listeners."You see, although I was born in Palestine, I spent most of my life in the United States. My father forced me back to this country to marry my cousin. My husband turned out to be worse than I expected. He mistreated me physically, emotionally, and verbally. Every day, his abuse increased and so I decided to end it today. I ran away because I couldn't take any more pain. I need to flee from this country at any cost, otherwise I would not have purposefully run into the Israeli forces," I said convincingly. "Dressed like a pauper, you don't appear like a traveler or from America."

"I just took off with little time to plan. Who cares how I look or what I'm wearing? I need help. Are you going to help me or lock me up?" I said impatiently. It was my appearance that always got me into trouble. It was either I was too pretty or purposely not pretty. I thought. Sometimes, I wanted to paint my face green so that my husband would just divorce me. I had my sanity to protect, and besides, he would have loved to claim me insane and still keep me in his dungeon of doom. I served as the best maid he and his parents ever could have. I cleaned, cooked, did their dirty laundry, and cared for his two little siblings. I was also a punching bag and his rape kit. When I slept, I was haunted by dramatizing nightmares. They were always about someone trying to kill me."Why should we believe you?"

"I'm an American citizen in a matter of life and death situation."

"You're lucky that one of my men didn't fire at you, charging at them the way you did," said the General, leaning forward with his head down and eyes rolled up. He was looking for my reply. "It's not like I was armed."

"By the time they knew that, you could have been dead," he said louder than before. "Joseph, did you find anything interesting in those papers?"

The good-looking man's face remained in the novel. I took one fast look at his crossed legs and noticed how one foot was pointed at my direction. I wondered how he managed to walk in that country without having his shoes full of dust or dirt. Without glancing at me, he turned his side to General Weisman. He rested my novel on his lap. He wore thin and clear yet stylish eyeglasses over his more-than-regular nose."I think you need to ask her more questions before letting her go," Joseph said as if I didn't exist in the room. "There is a situation here that you can't avoid, and you can't let her go back to them."

"Go where? If I don't leave here to the US, I'd rather die or get locked up," I interrupted. Both men looked at me with astonishment. I looked at the General and shifted my attention to Joseph. I finally got a good look at his face. He had well-structured features, his cheeks indented and his jawline defined. He had a fresh-out-of-the-shower scent mixed with ice-cool aftershave cologne. His green eyes resembled a deep and mysterious valley. I feared getting lost in them. I became startled as both men grilled me with their similar colored eyes. I hoped I didn't provoke their anger. I, on the other hand, possessed a pair of large midnight black-colored eyes. With naturally long eyelashes, mascara made me more powerful. I had a fair pale complexion due to the lack of sun exposure. I picked up many health tips from the West that I held on to wherever I went. For one thing, I took good care of my figure. That was the main thing that gave my family spite and jealousy. I fought against their feastly and over fattening foods. In the Middle East, they believe fatter means happier. Being thin meant being a sad and unhealthy person. The women valued cooking and serving it to their families. I hated cooking and wouldn't serve it unless pressured. When I spoke to my husband, I would receive a complimentary slap or push. However, with the two men in front me, I couldn't predict their actions or responses. "I think this young lady's unique issue should be treated accordingly with fair judgment," said Joseph. I thought that he had to have been an outsider. There was no way he lived in that country all his life and spoke perfect English as I did. He had no accent, and his speech flowed smoothly. I wondered where he had come from. A heavy and urgent knock at the door interrupted the debate. The soldier from behind the door didn't wait for permission. He opened the door and said, "Sir, you need to see this." He walked over to the television on the upper side corner of the office and turned it on. He put it on the same news channel that was in the other office. I couldn't understand the language being broadcasted. I did understand what was on anyway. Those were the familiar faces of my relatives and neighbors rallying, including my husband. He stood out from the crowd because he was carried on his best friend's shoulders. I was filled with confusion and fear. I feared my husband even though he was far. His appearance on television was as if he was in the same room with me. He was still hurting me in some way or another. I looked at General Weisman and then at Joseph for a translation of what was happening. The general stood up and walked over to the TV screen. Joseph looked at me and then turned to the TV screen eagerly. Suddenly, the two men faced me and I looked up at them for answers. "You are in bigger trouble than you thought, your people want your head. They claimed you worked for us," said General Weisman. "What do you mean, a spy?" I said, jumping off my seat. "That's ridiculous. I couldn't even spy on a cat." The General angrily walked over to his desk, picked up his phone, and dialed some numbers as if he was dialing through the phone with his thick fingers. Apparently, he was commanding some orders. Seconds later, he slammed it shut.

"I need to go and make sure this won't go out of hand. Can you stay and wait with her until I come back? You have time, right?" David Weisman addressed Joseph.

"Yes, I do, and I'll wait for you here. Besides, she appears harmless and innocent," Joseph said to David and took a quick glance at me and returned his sight to David in assurance. For the first time in my life, I had someone refer to me as innocent. That being said without me having to prove it sounded like a witness from heaven. I thought. In his eyes lived a deep sadness, different than mine.

CHAPTER THREE

Killer Looks

Joseph looked at me with his eyes squinting and a smirk on his face. He checked me out from head to toe, then his eyes landed on a rip in my pants. I forgot to fix the out of order buttoning my shirt. I felt filled with flaws and faults. "Why would a pretty woman like you get in a big ugly mess?" he said, resting his left elbow on the General's desk. I wasn't sure if he spoke in sarcasm. I didn't have much experience with Jewish people; they always appeared like aliens to me. Although at that point, I felt like an alien myself. I took a leap into another nation that I had little knowledge. All I was told in the past was how different we were and should remain. I wondered why the two nations disliked each other to such an extent. I remembered reading about the Jews in the Holy Quran that indicated many times that they were God's favorite race. It also stated that God gave them the whole world to freely live in. What went wrong? A big portion of the Quran talks about the children of Israel. A Muslim can name his children any name from the Jewish names, yet I wondered why they never named their children from our names. Maybe one day, they can. We used names such as Abraham, Joseph, Moses, Jacob, Isaac, were derived from the Israeli nation and many more. Yet I never heard a Jew name his child Mohamed or Ahmad, why?

"A Palestinian woman ran away to the enemy for help, such courage for a scared silly being," he provoked. "How can I be a coward if I'm a married Muslim woman alone with a Jewish man in one room." There went three rules broken. The first one I lied because fear ran in my blood. Second, a Muslim woman is prohibited from being alone with a strange man. Third and most dangerous, my marital status prohibited me from looking in another man's eyes. In that case, I found no resistance to prevent me from gazing into his eyes.

"You're a victim of your own circumstances," he said.

"No, their circumstances!" And I hated being referred to as a victim."If you say that you were forced to come to Israel or Palestine to wed, why didn't you report your case to the police over there?"

"Something you probably don't know and that is an Arabic girl tries and tries to prevent a forced marriage. When all else fails and everyone fails her, she doesn't step out of disobedience, regarding her authority figure."

Our conversation carried on like a court session. I felt like being put on a stand for not standing for myself. I became upset at Joseph because he acted like he knew all about the Muslim women. I felt even more complicated than any other. I had no time to elaborate and defend myself."The same figure killing her whole future, she disobeys and whatever the stakes are."

"Even if she was arranged at birth where the whole country helped throw her into it?"

"There is always another country that might just get her out," he said calmly.

"Or maybe you? Where were you all my life, sir?" Feeling all stirred up and battle mood was on.

"Where were you all those years sounds to me like a romantic cliché." I became certain that he came from America because only an American knew that line and wouldn't allow me to get away with it since I wrongly used it. I needed to stop the conversation from turning into a bigger fight. I stood up and walked over to the TV and turned it off. The news promoted my fear, especially in a foreign language. There was a deafening silence in the room.

"So why the bad ending?" Joseph asked.

"What are you talking about? What ending?"

"I meant the novel you wrote. Why did you end it so tragic? You seem like a fragile and delicate person, not brutal. I think your next novel should have a Cinderella theme." I couldn't believe that I felt flattered by that man and broke a hard-to-hide smile. I pressed my lips together, hiding my teeth. I remembered what my grandmother once told me. She said, "Never show any man your teeth when you smile, it only means you're cheap and easy."

"Cinderella died a long time ago. She doesn't exist, at least not in my book. I couldn't find the solution or a better ending for the two characters because I lived in such absolute misery," I said and felt the need to weep. I would have if he left the room. I went back to my seat and asked, "What was being said about me in the news? Please tell me. You seem like an intelligent and outspoken man." Flattery hit me again when he smiled at my remark. He sure didn't seem cheap to me when he smiled, revealing his straight and perfect white teeth.

"Although you may be in here, that doesn't mean you'll be leaving any time soon. Your husband made it more interesting. He said on the news that he wanted you dead or alive."

"Thanks for the reassurance," I said and tried to stop my eyes from tearing. I blinked repeatedly until I retrieved all the tears back into my eyes. I had to stop all speech with that man; I feared pain from his words. I don't know why I even cared what he had to say, but I did. I hardly spoke to or had long conversations with anyone, especially a man, a strange, out-of-my-world man.

"Your people are demanding that the Israeli police hand you over to them. It won't be long before all the press get a piece of you." He got my attention. I looked at him and tears just fell out my eyes. I had no idea why and how he brought out the hidden in me. I thought that the Israeli men were just as cruel as any men. Then again, I had to stop judging men because of one or a few bad encounters. I felt history may have made mistakes and misdirected people's relationships. I couldn't believe that a woman like me carried a normal non threatening conversation with a Jewish man and the world stood still. The misunderstandings among the Jews and the Muslims had exceeded beyond limit. It would take a miracle to have at least one from either side sit down or speak with care and good regards. I felt I just started a movement or a revolution. History changed before my eyes. A code had been broken and walls tumbled down as I felt confined in Joseph. A sudden feeling of nausea came over me. I ran to the basket by the door. I dropped to the floor and gushed out what had been settled in my stomach from the day before. I threw up vigorously and angrily. Joseph reacted with unexpected care. He put his gentle hand on my back as he squatted close to me. He surprised me with his touch that I shrieked and pulled away. He walked back to the desk and pulled out some tissues from my purse. He handed me the tissues and stood beside me till I stood up. He didn't appear the least bit disgusted. Only a doctor or a nurse would perceive another person's vomit as nothing. I feared that I may have hurt his feelings when I shrugged him off. I felt like falling in his arms and crying out all the tears in my heart. He seemed like a soft cushion that I wanted to rest my head on.

"That's my reflex to touch, I'm sorry," I said as I wiped my eyes, nose, and mouth. I carried the wastebasket and put it inside the General's private bathroom. With the door open, I washed my face.

I fixed my shirt. I wet my hair a little, hoping to look more combed. I wished I did dress better, and to show my American cool side, I felt I had someone new to impress.

"No need to apologize, I understand," he called out taking back his seat. His statement made me feel good for the first time in ages. I came out of the bathroom, feeling ashamed. He looked up at me and at my well-buttoned shirt. He seemed to take an interest in my case. I guessed there was no need to try to impress him after all. He didn't force me to. I forgot why I even threw up in the first place. Disappointing situations or recalling a bad event gave me that effect.

"I never said that we were going to hand you to them. Not if I can help it," he said with a changed tone and confidence. I felt comfortable and hopeful by the comment he delivered to my mind. I wished that it was a promise. A new type of trouble hit my heart, Joseph. "I see you know where my tissues are," I said and put my things back in my purse. I kept it on the desk till the General comes back and hands it back to me. Joseph handed me the novel and helped put it in my purse.

"What are you, I mean professionally, that is?" I had to ask. He wasn't a soldier or a detective.

"You see, David Weisman is my brother. I just stopped by to say good-bye to him before I leave. I came to Israel to witness my grandfather's burial," Joseph said with a sad tone.

"I'm sorry for your loss, and I'm sorry that you're leaving. Leaving to where?"

"If I tell, you might hate me," he said, and for the first time, he held his head down. For the first time, I hated the word hate. He hesitated and turned away. He also had issues of his own, which I became curious to invade. I didn't hate him; he gave me no reason to allow such a hard word to anchor. He used a familiar word among the population in that country. As for me, I had no hate, but disappointments.

"America? I knew it, no accent and the suit, it all fits. You must be some sort of professional."

"Yes, I'm an attorney at a firm located in New York City."

"Please get me out of here, take me with you, I know you have the right connections." I didn't believe in myself when I said that to him.

"Your case is not finished, and I have a lot on my plate as it is."

"I'm so stupid to even think you would accept my plea," I said as I smacked my forehead. Joseph leaned toward me and grabbed my hand tight. I felt his blood flow through his veins. My pulse increased in shock. He let go of my arm and appeared devastated. He stopped me from slapping my forehead as I normally did when faced with frustration.

"You must clear yourself here first, it might take time," he said as I felt time literally stop. His gaze cut through me like a butcher's knife. "If we were in New York, I'll represent you without consideration. I see many clients of domestic abuse, but I never practiced law here in this country. As we both know, rules here don't apply very well."

"I don't understand why they can't just follow one justice, one government."

"With justice and liberty for all?" he said and we both shared a unique and sad laugh. I had no recollection of the last time I shared a sincere and genuine laugh as that. We understood the world in a three-dimensional objective. Mine, his, and the other world we came from.

"Just wait and see if the General would release me once he comes back. I came willingly and should be able to leave as I wish." Joseph seemed to doubt that; he shook his head in disagreement. His forehead wrinkled, and his eyebrows fell close to his eyes. We both were caught off guard when the General rushed back in. He stopped and looked at us. Joseph retrieved back to his seat and sat straight.

We appeared guilty, yet unsure of what exactly.

"What happened here? Is she threatening you, Joseph?" the General asked. "No, she's enough threat to herself," Joseph said. "What's going on? Don't tell me those Palestinians actually think you're going to hand them Salwa." I loved the way he said my name. I felt a sense of existence. "Salwa? You sound like you know her to care about her," General Weisman jested. Joseph remembered my name from my passport, I assumed.

"So what time is your flight?" The General said coldly, it seemed he wanted to get rid of his brother out of our faces. The General had a new attitude, more personal.

"Don't worry about my flight, it can always wait for us." It was obvious Joseph wanted to make his brother's mood better. He seemed guilty to his brother for the moment.

"Salwa Adam, you made us look like fools. The press from Europe and the States are calling here for questions. Outside, you stirred up a riot. I had to put a new line of security to stop your people from causing any damage. They all ran home and scattered away once my men showed up. I had to use tear gas to get them all away. All that and for what? Nothing," said the General with less tolerance than before.

"When is the soul of a human being nothing? What does it take to be someone worth helping?"

"So what are you going to do?" Joseph asked his brother with concern for my state.

"That's my job. I'll take care of her, and you need to leave, Joseph."

"Don't kick me out and listen to me. I'm not leaving yet," Joseph said as he stood up and leaned closer to his brother. He was no doubt a lawyer. He seemed ready to defend something or someone or himself. He had a charismatic style, but his brother wasn't charmed.

"Aron, Mark!" the General called out loud. Two soldiers marched into the room quickly. "Take this woman and put her in a cell."

The two soldiers acted and gripped my arms. I looked at Joseph for a last chance and asked for help.

"Please, I never meant to bring any harm to anyone. I just needed to be saved from it." Joseph walked over to me and pulled me away from the two soldiers and asked them to leave. The General's face was ready to pop like a red balloon. He was angered, and there was no telling what he was going to do. "I said take her to the cell, until I figure out what to do with her, now!" he yelled louder.

Joseph tried to fight for my humanitarian state. I felt like a yo-yo from one hand to another. I started to face the door and head out of the office, but the tension increased. Their voices were heard by the rest of the Israelis outside the office. It appeared as though I caused a riot inside and outside."You better leave, Joseph, and just let me do my job here," said the General."You don't know what you're doing. She's asking us for help and what do you do?" Joseph's voice became louder. "We are not in New York, Counselor!" said the General and slammed his palm on the desk. He seemed serious and would take it further; therefore, fear won with me again. Joseph lost his cool and put a fight for me. He blocked me from leaving that room before he could understand what would become of my case. His eagerness defeated my fear. The General had more power and control; he walked over to the door and faced his brother. I hated violence of any sort, and I couldn't stand to watch the problem escalate. I reached for the door and opened it for myself and the other two soldiers. Joseph couldn't prevent me from stepping out. Therefore, I made things easier for all of them. He held my arm as I reached for the doorknob; I let him down gently and proceeded to exit. It felt like a burning oven, and I felt like I was the roast chicken. Leaving that office took a lot from me; I left a new and exceptional friend behind and maybe forever. Sometimes, change needed to wait before any effects can go through. I felt enriched to have an Israeli man stand up for me and against his own brother and government. Not to be taken lightly, but I felt as if Joseph had saved me already, regardless of my stay in a cell. Loyalty came in a different package than anyone could ever handle. I made up my mind to respect Joseph for as long as I lived. His true colors were shown, and he had no reason to deny me. He killed me with his niceness; it took a man to defend a weak woman, but it took a greater man to attempt helping me, that man was Joseph.

CHAPTER FOUR

A Helping Handful

The tension grew out of hand as I was escorted to my new cage and was deposited in it. I saw Joseph race out of his brother's office. He seemed very upset and hurt. To me, he was moving in slow motion. The world stopped rotating because there was a new axis that my world rotated around. He looked like a black knight. It was easy to picture him with a fluttering black cape. He passed by and gave me an indefinite glance. I felt alone and empty as he left the building. In my cell, I sat down on the small bed with disgust. I was an expert cleaning lady. I imagined how I would polish that cell and get rid of the awkward unpleasant smell. I felt faint before I received something to eat. With nothing better to do, my resentment for my father grew. As much as I was to blame for being in that prison, I still felt it was his entire fault. He drove me to that.

Last year, I begged him to have me return to America and see my youngest sister's wedding. After exhausted efforts, he accepted.

He allowed me only two weeks' stay. I tried to never come back to Palestine/Israel, but as usual, he won. He cut me off from society and took away my life. I was a slave in my own home. He shoved me back to his nephew for his own older brother's sake. I warned him that one day I would break away from that marriage he tied me to.

I felt very misinformed in the Israeli headquarters and puzzled. I wondered if Joseph had disappeared from my life forever. I preferred staying in the small cell than returning to Sammy. The things he would have done to me if he gets his hands on me, I was afraid to imagine. I also felt more lost because I had no idea what was happening on my behalf inside and outside the headquarters. I shut my eyes to rest and fell asleep on the dirty mattress. I was suddenly woken up by a strange soldier who charged in and asked me to get up. My heart jumped out of my body; I stood up without any delay. He was carrying a command and didn't care to say anything else to me. I felt suspicious of him because he wouldn't look at me. He wore dark shades in the evening in a building. He also wore the red soldier's hat. He wasn't armed with any weapons like the other soldiers. He held me by my arm. He held a black bag with his other. He walked swiftly and silently. We passed through the long hallway and away from all the offices I've been to earlier that day. He took me to the ladies' room and ordered me to wear the uniform in the black bag.

"Put this on and hurry, we don't have much time," he whispered.

"I'm scared to get into more trouble, no, I won't. I can't escape from the General. I would definitely be confirmed guilty without charge." He lifted his shades and then I recognized those eyes. It was Joseph! I feel that I must have been dreaming.

"Don't worry about the General, I'll take care of him later," he said with diligence. I felt a rush of excitement and inspiration. I recklessly changed into the soldier's uniform Joseph had given me. He waited by the door like a bodyguard. I was shocked to find my purse was also included in that black bag.

"Look at you, soldier," he said, fixing my collar, forcing me to smile.

"I'm definitely dead meat, or going to be," I said as we both marched like imposters. Joseph told me to walk normal and put up a straight posture from that point on. I felt a sweet taste of rebellion. We safely exited the building despite the heavy security scattered by the gates. He waved good-bye to the last soldier and gave him a wink and a smile. I wasn't sure what our next move would be. I couldn't help but trust Joseph. Although trust was something I rarely felt. My life was in his hands. He went through all the trouble to get me out. My admiration for him increased. A sense of adventure and danger was pumped into my heart and soul.

CHAPTER FIVE

Historic Drive-Through

Joseph and I were met by a young female soldier. She had short black hair and fair complexion. I hoped that she was his sister or relative.

"Salwa, this is my sister Rachel," Joseph introduced her quickly. I was glad that she was his sister and at the same time relieved. Rachel was waiting for us in a two-door Honda car. Joseph helped me inside, and he came and sat next to me. I was surprised because in my culture, the man drives while the oldest passenger takes the front passenger seat.

"You are a very beautiful woman, Salwa, even in a soldier's uniform," Rachel said, as if she has ever seen me in any other clothing. The comment was unexpected and ended up causing my face to turn red.

"You're making her blush," Joseph said, trying to look at my face. I turned away and looked at the road. Rachel was a speed driver. Her driving reminded me of Brooklyn residents. In Brooklyn, even a yellow traffic light means go to them. If you stay more than two seconds after it turns green, you'll have everyone beeping their horns and bad mouths. We all became serious when we were stopped by the Israeli police by the intersection. Prior to entering any city or town, there would always be security officials asking for identification and a possible inspection of the vehicle if the part appeared suspicious. Joseph spoke in his charming tone in Hebrew to the soldier, distracting him from looking inside the car. We proceeded with the two men laughing, waving friendly good-byes.

"That was close," Rachel sighed with relief.

"Rachel, stop by that cuisine restaurant, I want to get us something to eat for later. Salwa, how would you like to eat some falafel and hummus with vegetable salad? I think we all can agree on that."

"Sounds good as long as you go vegan on me. But I really don't think we should be making any stops. I'm scared of getting reported or caught," I said, reminding him of my double runaway position. "I'll jump in and out, will only take a minute," Joseph insisted. He ran out of the car quickly and into the store. Rachel turned around and looked at me. She had a secret smile on her face, only a woman knew. "Joseph is sweet, but he does crazy things sometimes," she said in search of my opinion. "He's brave and a real man indeed," I said, proud of what he has done for me so far. We were crossing a historical line, forbidden by law and nature. An Israeli man helping a Palestinian woman escape from his own government. Who knew what the future had in store for our dangerous attempt. "I never saw him this crazy though, and I can't believe I'm helping him do this either," Rachel said.

"Sometimes, doing the exceptional and extraordinary thing may appear crazy. I think Joseph must have a great deal of guts," I said. Joseph jumped back into the car with a bag of fresh cooked food. "Go, drive away, Rachel," he said while putting the bag on the floor between us. The fresh fried falafel was mesmerizing. The smell filled the car, and I couldn't wait to sit for the most amazing feast of my life.

"Where are we going?" I asked, turning to Joseph. He didn't seem to be worried at all.

"We're going home," he said mysteriously. I wasn't sure what home meant. Was it his home in Tel-Aviv or America or my husband's home?

"I've got everything planned, don't worry," Joseph said as he leaned forward to his sister.

"Grandma is not thrilled about all this," he said to Rachel.

"I explained the situation to her and asked her for help," Rachel said smiling.

"I got the two tickets ready, they're at home." "Are we leaving this country?" I asked them with anticipation like a little girl who is expecting a pony.

"You guys are, I want to stay a little longer with Grandma, and then I'll leave," Rachel said, looking at me in the back view mirror.

"You don't live here either?" I asked Rachel. "She's an American citizen, like you and me, also a New Yorker," Joseph said as we all laughed. We drove through the city. Then we stopped near a house with a beautiful front garden. There were trees and flowers. Some fruit and vegetable trees surrounded the front gates. Small ripe tomatoes caught my eye as we all walked up the few steps to the door. Joseph reached for one and plucked it; he handed it to me. "Tomatoes are my favorite," I said. Joseph was encouraged to pluck out some more and gave them to me. He tossed one in his mouth. In Tel-Aviv, I felt like a runaway fugitive. I was afraid to be found by my people and by Joseph's people. Caught between two worlds, they have been at war for years. I gave them something new to share in common. They would both be hunting me down. I thought to myself. I felt that the world would detest my moves, but they lacked the knowledge of my motives. I enjoyed the company of new friends and hoped for us to escape without any difficulty.

CHAPTER SIX

Best Feast!

Joseph, Rachel, and I were welcomed by an old lady dressed in black. She had a gray bun on the back of her head. She had a hunchback. She seemed to be about eighty years old, at least, I thought. Her hard of hearing made it hard to communicate with her without the authorities breaking in on us. Joseph laid out the food on the table and Rachel helped automatically. She ran back and forth, providing dishes and cups of water.

"We need to eat fast, change our clothes, and head to the airport. Our plane takes off in two hours," Joseph said to me as he took a seat by my side. I was filled with admiration for everyone at that table, including the grandmother. I ate in silence as my tears fell down my face. I felt like an orphan, and for the first time, I found a temporary loving home. Joseph stopped eating and comforted me, "You're going to be just fine, soon, you'll be home eating with your family in New

York," he said. Little did he know that they would have me for dinner after what I have done.

"I'm touched by your kindness and efforts. I can't thank you all enough."

"Salwa, I have the perfect outfit for you, I'm sure it'll fit. You and I are not that much different in body type. I may be a few pounds extra, but I'm working on it."

"You're always working on it," said Joseph, forcing everyone to laugh. Rachel took me by the hand to her room and advertised in a showcasing mode the new clothes to me. It was a black suit with pink undershirt, pink sleeves, and collar. My favorite color pink represented beauty and happiness to me. She left me alone to change into my new clothes. I loved how elegant and comfortable they fit. I wondered what Joseph would be wearing in the other room. I finally had a decent brush to brush my hair from the knots. I added a little touch of makeup on my face. Rachel gave them to me to keep. I put them in my purse. I looked in the mirror before stepping out of the room and I shocked myself. I never felt a glow as I did or prettier, not even on my wedding day. Rachel runs into the room and hands me a pair of medium heeled shoes."Now you're perfect," she said, amazed at the outcome she had contributed. I took a deep breath before exiting the bedroom and looked for Joseph's reaction. He dressed faster than I did. He wore a suit that made him look like a model. He had the flattest abs I ever saw on a man. His broad shoulders gave him a masculine appeal. Even with my new medium sized heels, he appeared taller than me.

"Arabian princess, I'm at your service," Joseph bowed. That moment he took my breath away and swept me off the face of the earth. Rachel pushed Joseph out of the way. They seemed to have a friendly bondage. His easy and free spirit made the situation amusing. Joseph fixed his tie and fixated his deep eyes on me. After losing track of time, I remembered to pull my gaze away. I smiled and hid behind his sister. Rachel handed me my ticket and passport. "How much do I owe you?" I asked Rachel.

"I didn't pay for them, I charged it on my brother's account. He's the one you should pay."

"It's on the house," Joseph jumped in between us. His generosity made me feel valuable almost priceless. I put them in my pocket on the left side of my chest pocket. She put Joseph in his suit jacket pocket as he went to lift his shoulder suitcase. Joseph kneeled to say his good-bye to his grandmother who was still seated at the table. She caressed his soft black hair. I walked over and said loudly, "Thank you, Grandma, for everything." Joseph looked up at me pleased.

"Take good care of yourself, and don't get yourself into any more trouble. Kiss the children for me, and inform me of your wife's condition every chance you get.

"I felt disappointed and almost heartbroken upon hearing that Joseph had a wife. Why wouldn't he? I thought and focused on my departure. I walked away and acted as if I didn't just hear what the grandmother said. The phone rang and everyone was driven with fear, Joseph suggested not pick up. We raced out of that house like a gang. Rachel drove us to the Tel-Aviv airport. We got out of the car. I gave Rachel a warm hug and said, "Thank you so much, I hope I can pay you back some day."

"We'll have coffee and doughnuts in New York someday. I know how to find you," she said and added, Joseph would help me if I can't."

"Take care," she said to Joseph, giving him a quick hug and a kiss on his cheek. We made no eye contact with the heavy security at the airport. We were two guilty travelers with a lot to risk. She drove away without any hesitation.

CHAPTER SEVEN

Airport Threat

We walked to the checking clerk for our bag inspection. We had nothing illegal to hide in those bags. We proceeded to the ticket booth to check our tickets. We were almost free before an army of soldiers marched into the airport along with the General. We were surrounded by armed soldiers and terror.

"What do you think you're doing?

Joseph, you went against my orders," said the General as he approached his brother and stood parallel faced.

"Let us go, I beg you. You know she's not guilty of any crime," Joseph whispered to his brother. "You broke my rules and kidnapped her from my headquarters. Unless you want me to charge you too, I suggest you leave right now."

"What are you going to do, arrest me? Go ahead. If she goes, I go, "Joseph said. The pressure grew as the people watched with fascination. I feared the Muslims in that airport would recognize me from the news and make things worse. No one moved because of the intimidating security. "Arrest me because I'm the one who kidnapped her against her will and I'm taking her to the US," Joseph said while blocking me from David Weisman. "Why are you ruining your life for her? If you keep defending her, you're going to lose everything," Weisman said in displeasure. "Did you forget who you are and what she is?"

"She's a victim and I'm doing what I do best, defending and helping the innocent."

"This is just the beginning of your problems. Back away from her and don't make me embarrass you. Before you know it, you will lose your job," said Weisman. He looked around at his men and held his hand out to stay away from Joseph and me. "I'll come with you even though I don't know what crime I have committed," I said walking from behind Joseph. I faced the General. I hated being the source of Joseph's quarrelling with his brother. Joseph stopped me from getting any closer to his brother. The airport was like a movie scene, the public watched with amazement. Eventually, passengers were forced to leave the scene when their flight was called for departure. I heard our airplane when it called for its passengers to take off. I became worried and feared missing our flight. We were close to ending everything had we not been stopped by the General.

"It would look good on your behalf that you helped an American citizen escape the turmoil of her people, especially if she was a Muslim. It's nothing personal, but pure politics. What do you say?" The General looked at me and seemed to realize that I may have a good point. He took one step backward.

"David, please let us by, you won't regret it," Joseph pleaded from his heart to his brother. David seemed to be considering the plea. He took a deep breath and blew from his mouth.

"Joseph, take care of yourself, I just wanted what's best for you. I hope your stubbornness benefits you." Weisman looked at his men and ordered them out. He gave his brother a warning gaze and said, "Farewell, little brother." Joseph leaped over his firm postured brother and gave him a rough embrace. David Weisman appeared motionless, yet gave a small smile for one second. He turned around, keeping his pride and attitude intact. Joseph picked up his bag and I picked up mine, and we both were admitted into the airplane passenger's gate.

CHAPTER EIGHT

What Goes Up?

We entered the airplane with a sense of victory, smiled, and kept passing through the airplane in search of our seats. I ignored all the eyes that were focused on us and walked in front of Joseph as the crowd made space for us. Some appeared standing as if they were deliberately giving us a standing ovation. "Keep going until you find our marked seats, you can have a seat by the window," Joseph said as we made it through to our designated seats.

"Aren't you nice?" I said as I took it without negotiating. I feared that the General might change his mind about me leaving Israel. I also feared anyone from my town might be on that flight. Security was still far from my reach. I hated to think of my father's reaction and how he would handle my escape. With little baggage, I decided to keep my purse with me. Joseph reached for the storage compartment and put his case in it. Before he took his seat, he took off his jacket. He folded it neatly and put it in his lap as he took the middle seat right next to me. Later, he laid his jacket by the empty seat. My heart jumped when he dropped himself in his seat. I felt the danger of his closeness. It would be impossible to make it legal. Our different religions always lived in segregation among each other. There we were two American citizens with extremely opposite identities in sync. We had no care for our separate pasts and aimed at a similar destination. I pulled open the shade to my window and took a longing last look at the mesmerizing city. Its beauty mystified the world. How I wished that the two nations would settle their differences. Instead, they acted like a big dysfunctional family where no one got along. Always fighting and quarrelling with nothing gained. The city seemed ever so beautiful. I guessed that the only time you appreciate something when you feel you're about to leave it. I had no intention of ever returning to that country, not to the same situations at least. Israel and Palestine were two nations that agreed to never agree. Many politicians tried and failed to issue a peace plan. I dreamt many times of finding the solution for the populations in that Holy Land. Joseph leaned in and shared the view with me. "It seems quiet and safe from here," he said. "Yet secrets that lie in the grounds are more dangerous than the ones walking on that land

"I just wish that those people just accept one another's existence and differences without trying to conquer one another," I said with a sigh. "That's what interested me in you, you dare to dream of building a bridge that connects the two dangerous nations," Joseph said.

"You read my mind?"

"I didn't, I read your novel, remember?"

"Oh, that story," I said, remembering how he did read into it with fascination.

"That's how I knew a little about you and your heart. You're a unique woman and deserve to be cared for," he said. "You're a good writer, I must add, I'm afraid to say without you thinking wrongly of me, also beautiful."

"I thought he had to be the sweetest thing ever to even care enough of how I took a compliment. His kind words made me nervous. I shifted his attention to buckling up the seat belts. I wrestled with mine and my thumb ached as I tried to buckle my seat belt. "Ouch!" I snapped."What happened to your thumb and palm?" Joseph asked. I felt like he knew. I always had a hard time talking about my husband's abuse to anyone."Kitchen hazardous; baking caused it," I joked. He knew I concealed the truth. I couldn't wait for the airplane to take off. I felt like flying it at full speed. I would not rest till it took off from the ground. I wanted to fly in space. I tightened my fists in anticipation."When would it fly already?"

"You're such a New Yorker," Joseph said, smiling. "They want everything fast. They eat fast foods, drive fast cars, and take on fast tasks."

"What about you, aren't you a New Yorker?"

"I didn't say I wasn't."

Some passengers cheered as the airplane took a long stride on the runway. I wanted to cheer loudest, but my shyness restricted me. I finally escaped my old life and had no idea what awaited me. I dreaded meeting my father, and worst, I feared his torment. I turned my head to look out the window while in deep thought. I had no armor against his anger and fury. I risked going back to his prison.

"What are you worried about?" Joseph interrupted my deep thoughts. I didn't want to reveal my fears. Yet I knew he knew the answer to his provocative question. I wanted him to think I'll be alright. I had to push him away for his own good. I couldn't keep depending on him, although there was nothing more I needed. He gave me security and contentment."I'm just thinking of how happy my family would be to see me," I said.

"You think they'll be okay with you? You ran away from your husband. He charged you with being a spy in the media, and now you're riding with a Jewish man."

"A friend is a friend, it doesn't matter who or what."

"A Jewish friend is a bit heavy for them to carry," he invoked. "Once I explain the situation, they'll understand," I said. I felt that he could see through me. He allowed me to cover the truth to spare me the pain. Joseph changed the subject to something more productive and promising. "I think you should publish your novel as soon as you can."

"You really believe that anyone would like it?" I asked in denial.

"I loved it, and I don't read novels. I'll help you publish it."

"As much as that sounded great, I couldn't afford to stay connected to him."I'm sorry, but it's a big risk. I don't know how to hide you from my family and others."

"Give me a proxy to work everything out for you, I'm a lawyer and I have many friendly connections. I want you to be rich, then no one would dare push you around, not even your father," he said, acknowledging my source of torture. "How would we communicate? Not by phone, I'm afraid they would be tapped."

"Just hand me that story and trust me," he said confidently. I reached into my purse and gave it to him. He unbuckled the seat belt. He stood up and went to his suitcase in the storage closet over our heads. He opened it and fixed my paper book over his things. He took back his seat happily. He reached for his notepad and pen. He wrote out a proxy and asked me to sign it after he did. I had nothing to lose. He put his notepad away in his jacket's inner pocket, where he got it in the first place. That was my first business deal. I felt rich before I became rich. He promised to pay for the extra needed expenses regarding publishing and marketing. I told him that I can't afford to pay him. He made me agree to pay him back if I made over a million dollars."I know you will and then you can pay me only what I spent just to make you happy." How could he blindingly believe in me? I wondered.

"If you don't mind me asking, but why do you wear your wedding ring on your right hand finger?" I had to know.

"Are you asking me if I'm married?" He asked with a half smile on his face. He looked like James Bond for a moment when he lifted one of his eyebrows. "I'm just curious," I said in defense.

"I've been married for six years, and I have two children, a boy and a girl. Unfortunately, my wife is battling chronic and fatal cancer. She's been suffering from it for four years now."

"I'm really sorry to hear that, and forgive me for asking."

"I've been caring for her only. That's how our relationship has been going on for three years. I take her in and out of hospitals."

"No wonder you carry so much compassion in your heart. That's the reward you get for caring for the sick. You have that sympathy and light that marks your goodwill."

I felt sorry for reminding him of a buried pain. He also had a broken heart, yet he was filled with love and tenderness. The stewardess passed by with a snack cart. I feared that Joseph would reach for the alcohol drink he ordered. His hand extended toward the glass cup, then turned to me and rejected it. He made a considered decision in being sensitive to my religion. In my culture, we are prohibited from drinking any form of alcoholic beverages or any intake of alcohol-based food products. It pleased me to know that Joseph turned down his drink out of respect and with full knowledge of my disregard for it. Instead I recommended two hot and rich cups of coffee. I liked mine black, while he added milk to his. "Cheers, to a new life!" Joseph said as his cup slightly tapped mine. We drank our coffee in heavenly bliss. We didn't need caffeine to keep us awake. Hours passed like minutes, and I never spoke so much in a single sitting than I had in those few hours with Joseph. We discussed politics, religion, movies, and music. He tried to understand why I was a vegetarian. He failed at making me convert to red and white meats. I grew up in poverty and meat was never properly introduced or prepared. Rejecting it all at once made me build a stronger resistance to anything else that appeared unattainable. Although we had odd tastes in everything, yet those were the things that kept our conversations going. We realized we had nothing in common, yet opposites attract in chemistry. After the caffeine finished its effect, I felt warm and safe to drift away in a peaceful drift. I took a short nap, and when I woke up, I found Joseph's jacket on my chest. It smelled clean with a hint of aftershave cologne. Joseph had also taken a nap. I took his jacket off me and covered him with it. The captain announced that we were close to landing. I stared at Joseph for a long while with his eyes closed. He faced my direction and rested his head on a small pillow. To me, he was the eighth wonder of the world. I never met anyone with that much magnetic force. I enjoyed watching him and didn't have the heart to ruin his restful sleep. I monitored his breathing and his angelic face. I sketched a vivid image of his face and carved in my psych. I nearly jumped out of my seat when, all of a sudden, he opened his eyes wide. "I caught you, very intriguing!" he said, laughing. I didn't mind being the reason for his long laugh. I resisted joining him in his laughter for my bust.

"I needed to make sure of something," he said after catching me in a guilty pleasure of gazing at him. "How long were you awake?"

"Long enough to know that—"A loud scream came from a woman seated a few rows behind us. Joseph and I looked over for the noise. One man stood by our seat and looked at Joseph and me in disgust. He had a gun in his hand and aimed our direction. The angry gunman caused a panic all around him. With nowhere to run but to the arms of death, I complied. I took his order to stand up. Joseph pulled me down. I let go of him and stood up again. "Stop and let me see what he wants!" I shouted at Joseph. I hoped to make him mad, so he would remain seated. I tried to make him mad, so he would fight me and not the gunman for his own good. "I don't need you, stay here or you'll die here," said the gunman to Joseph. He pointed his gun right at Joseph's temple. I jumped right between them. I distracted the gunman from Joseph's attention. Joseph grabbed my right arm from behind me; I ignored him and looked at the gunman's face. I shrugged Joseph's grip and walked ahead of the gunman quickly so that he would follow. I gave peaceful eye contact to those that captured my eyes. The same eyes I neglected earlier for fear of recognition. That time, I meant to tell them that everything would be fine since I was the one the gunman needed anyway. Some women were ready to cry. I forced myself to pass a grin to calm them down. I felt the metal gun on my spine and made sure it stayed there so that he wouldn't panic and shoot recklessly at the other passengers. As soon as Joseph stood up, the gunman turned around and struck him with the back of the gun on his forehead, knocking Joseph back to his seat. A few loud yet short shrieks were heard and immediately silenced. I stumbled on the seat and sat while looking at the gunman, "Why are you doing this? You're making a big mistake, you can't get away with this," I said in a warning tone.

"Why did you do what you did? You're a spy for the enemy, and you're traveling with your lover who's a Jew. You're a disgrace to our country, and killing you slowly would be my pleasure."

"You mean oppressing me. You're not a hero, you're a coward and what will you get out of it when I do die, nothing!" I said, challenging him. "The truth would be out while you rot in jail in regret. I'm nobody's enemy and nobody's lover either!" I said, he seemed to reflect for a moment.

Men intimidated me, with or without a gun. I couldn't even put up a fair fight if I tried."You sold yourself cheap, that's what your hometown said about you," he said, waving the gun at me with one hand and wiping the sweat off his forehead with the other.

"I never sold anything, it's me who got sold for cheap!" I said as I hit a painful core. I cried and put my head down. I felt the airplane taking a dive. It felt faster than normal, which led to a sudden drop to the ground. The gunman lost complete balance and a bullet shot flew out of his gun. He went tumbling down to the floor in front of me. Two male passengers rose from their seats and tackled the gunman. Joseph charged toward us. He sat on the gunman's belly punching him out of control. I couldn't move, I thought, out of shock. I noticed horror and derangement in Joseph's eyes as he turned to look at me. He stopped hitting the gunman and rubbed his hair intensely. He frowned and appeared weaker than a few seconds ago. He crawled over to my knees and started crying out loud.

"You've been shot! Oh no, I'm sorry I couldn't stop him." I looked at my abdomen and noticed the blood oozing in abundance. I wondered how I didn't feel the bullet when it struck me. I felt Joseph's genuine concern. The passengers of the airplane gathered around me and some cried while others buried their faces either in their hands or in another's arms. Joseph helped me take off my jacket; he folded it and compressed it on the bleeding area. His face turned red and wet from tears. He had a fresh bruise on his temple. "How many times do I have to die before I die?" I said in despair.

"You're not going to die, it's a simple wound."

With the help of other passengers, he stretched me flat on the two seats. I saw the gunman being taken away by four men. His face bled as well from all the beating from Joseph and the other men. I could only hear Joseph's breathing and his heartbeat. It was the first time I felt someone's extreme compassion toward me. His nose touched mine as he tried to talk me out of fainting. His nose may have been bigger than average, but to me, it was the most beautiful feature I acknowledged on him. Death had to be sweet having that many caring faces around me, I thought.

"Please don't give up!, I promise to make things better for you. You don't deserve this," Joseph desperately spoke to keep me conscious and awake. I woke up from a slight and gentle tapping on my face. I wanted to fall asleep and deny all that had happened. I felt pressure added to my wound. That made it uneasy to fall back to unconsciousness. With a faded image, I noticed Joseph's exhausted efforts to stop my bleeding. "Come on, Salwa, fight back!," Joseph said. Sweat and tears covered his face. It was amazing how those few words gave me strength and hope.

It seemed that the airplane had come to a complete stop. I noticed unfamiliar faces looking at me with revulsion. I looked at my pink shirt; it was stained with red blood. I felt like crying, but I didn't. I fell in a daze as I thought of my father. I feared he would blame me for all that has happened to me. Worst of all, if the rumors reached him, he would have me disowned. It would be an easy way out for him. He didn't like to deal with real issues. He would not waste time to help me clear my name. Joseph's hand held my face, and he took me out of my worrisome gaze. His eyes turned red and diminished the beauty of his green pupils. "It's not your fault, you're an innocent woman. I promise to defend you," he insisted strongly. That's when I broke into tears. He uttered the most healing statement ever given to any human being. He knew what worried me. A medical crew raced in the tight area I lay on the airplane. Joseph moved quickly to my shoulder's side, allowing room for them to give me proper care. "You know, just when I thought that you and I might be the reason for changing the relations between Israel and Palestine, I go and get dying."

"Don't be silly, you're not dying, and we will change the views of the world and generations to come, together."

CHAPTER NINE

Gunned Down

America did help Joseph and I become friends. If we were both raised and lived all our lives in Israel, I think we would have been holding each other's necks. Sometimes, stepping out of the box makes you see things for what they really are.

A nightmare took me out of my restful stage. I saw myself being taken to my family's house. My mother allured me into a strange room. She looked scary, but I followed her anyway. She had a brand-new wooden coffin on a table. She made me go in it. Then she started choking me with her bare hands. I looked over her shoulders and noticed my father standing with his hands behind his back. My brothers stood by him. My sisters stood along his other side. I wanted to scream for help, but the choking disabled my voice box. I almost tasted death when I felt my chest jump up from a cardiac pump machine. "We've got her, welcome back, Ms. Adam," said a middle-aged male doctor dressed in scrubs. He appeared like a medical ninja. A loud and excited cheer filled the operating room. Moments later, I fell asleep again. A thrusting pain in my abdomen made my heart rate beat faster. I opened my drowsy eyes and noticed a crowd of medical staff running around in a big room. I had IV tubes connected to my left arm. I felt an excruciating pain and called out to the nearest nurse, "Where am I?"

"You're in the intensive care unit, very soon we'll take you to your own room," said the nurse.

"Can I have something for the pain?" I asked.

"I'll have to consult with the doctor first, hang on, I'll be right back."

Surprised to be alive, confusion filled my mind. I wondered how long I had been there. I also wondered how much longer I needed to stay there. I did not know what to expect outside that hospital or inside. Apparently, no visitors were allowed. I received specific care from a sweet old nurse. She tugged me with the cotton covers, helped elevate my head with a soft pillow, and gave friendly smiles. A doctor came shifting toward me. The same doctor I saw previously. He approached me eagerly, "How are you feeling, Ms. Adam?" he asked.

"I feel like I just had my stomach popped," I said.

"It's not that bad, nothing we couldn't fix," he said as he inserted some medications from a syringe into the IV tube. I felt the pain subside gradually. "You're a fascinating patient, you have a crowd of people dying to get their hands on you," he said in admiration.

"I don't want to see anyone," I said to the doctor.

"I want to see you!" said Joseph, forcing himself into the room. He shrugged off the two nurses advising him to keep away. "How are you doing?" he asked as he leaned closer and smiled. He seemed like a wreck. His shirt had spots of blood on it. His tie hung loose around his neck. The unshaved hair on his face made him appear restless. "How did you get in here, sir? No one is allowed in the ICU yet."

"It's alright, Doctor, he's my cousin," I said, trying to sit up. "Please allow him to stay for a moment and then I'll kick him out." The doctor agreed unhappily and walked out of the room.

"Cousin? Is that the best you could come up with?" Joseph said as he grabbed a chair and moved it by my bedside. He sat with a sigh of relief. He transformed into a person with a lively and energetic attitude.

"Technically, Jews and Muslims are considered cousins in my religion's point of view."

"Most people either don't know or forget that information, it's such a shame." I felt a rich feeling in my heart, having Joseph by my side. His compassion made the pain tolerable. We both looked at each other with so much to say. We knew words couldn't express our situation. The dangers that may rise from our friendship couldn't be denied. "Don't you have to be home, and how about your job, your family?" I said, trying to push him away.

"I need to make sure that you're okay first, really, how are you feeling?" he asked.

"I'm fine and you need to get out of here fast. It won't be long before my family comes here to check on me, and I'm afraid that they might hurt your feelings or you in general," I said.

"We are in America now, with different rules and rights," he said, pushing his glasses close to his eyes.

"I can't argue with a lawyer," I said. A stampede of people came barging into the ICU. I caught my breath when I noticed my father, mother, two brothers, and two sisters charging in toward me. Joseph instantly stood up and took a few steps away from my bed. "Who the hell is this?" my oldest brother asked, looking at Joseph.

"He is my lawyer," I said, stopping Joseph from replying. With one against six, I wished Joseph would forfeit and withdraw himself from the scene. "Since when do you need a lawyer?" asked my oldest sister.

"Do you have any idea what you have caused us in humiliation?" my father said. "Is this the man you were with?" My father implied in a slanderous tone. He walked over to Joseph and seized him by his shirt.

My brother threw a punch at Joseph's jaw line. My other brother tied Joseph's two arms behind him.

"Stop it, just stop!" I shouted as I reached for my emergency button and secretly rang it. A few nurses ran into the room to stop a fight from taking place; one ran out yelling, "Security!"

"You're making a big mistake with your accusations. Your daughter is a victim, and maybe you should try to help her instead of making things worse," Joseph said loudly. He broke away my father's hands and my brothers'. The same time, two security men walked in. "I want you out of our life," my father said as a security man dragged him out and proceeded out of the room. The other security man tried to sweep the rest of the crowd. My sisters frowned at me and showed no care for my condition. My mother looked at me with mistrust. My father claimed total ownership of me and refused to leave the room easily. I guessed wrong in him disowning me. I felt deeply saddened and disappointed in my dysfunctional family. I put my head down in embarrassment and gave Joseph a secret glance. I meant to tell him that I did warn him of that. The room felt like a volcano. I feared that the fighting would erupt again or later. Joseph looked at me, wiping his bleeding lip from the punch he just took for my sake. "Joseph, thank you for everything, and you need to stop right here, right now," I said, crying. He looked at me with amazement. Joseph stood silent and appalled. He waited until everyone else had evacuated the room. He walked closer and sat beside me on the bed. "You can't surrender your right to have someone defend you, mark my words, I won't ever give up until I know you're 100 percent safe and happy."

"If you want to remain alive, get out of my life," I said, stuttering. "Your life is my life now," he said. I felt electrified as he leaned in and kissed my cheek. After that we were sealed by that divine peck.

He flew out of the room with that same imaginary cape only I see on him. My tears declined and my heart fluttered. I remained gazing at the ceiling for a while and then closed my eyes. My family members were barred from visiting me. I woke up again and found myself in a beautiful private hospital room. With my bed next to the window, I looked up at the skies. A large and serious looking man walked in after a heavy knock. He didn't wait for my permission to enter. A more timid smaller framed man followed. Each man wore a suit with a tie and a suspicious look on their faces. "Hello, Ms. Adam, I'm Detective Harrison and this is my partner Detective Smith. We need to ask you a few questions about the shooting incident, if you don't mind," he said as he reached to shake my hand. He gave me no time to object, he went on aggressively. "Have you ever seen the shooter before, or do you know him?"

"It's a long story and I don't think this is the right time to discuss such details," I said, trying to remain at peace. I dropped my head back at my pillow and pulled up my blanket. I turned my head away to the open curtain of my window.

"Your case is a federal issue, and it is important that you cooperate with us," he said, reaching for the single seat couch. He sat with one leg crossed over the other. He opened his notepad with one hand and held a pen with the other hand. He didn't seem to take no for an answer. He intimidated me with his loud voice and overconfident posture. His partner, Smith, pulled another chair on the other side and sat in it. He seemed more respectable than Mr. Harrison. He sat humbly and confidently as well. Both men were eager to find out more information."No, I never saw the shooter before, and I didn't know him until he shot me," I said. I disliked discussing the details of the matter. It took on an emotional effect on me. I wondered why someone would hate me enough to shoot me. I would never hate anyone and even dare to think of hurting them.

"Why did he shoot you?" he asked."I don't know, and I don't care," I said in frustration. I hoped that would end our conversation. "Before coming here, I had the privilege of doing a little research on you. You were a popular topic in Israel, weren't you?"

"In what form?" I asked curiously. "I'll tell you what I know if you promise to answer all my questions," he bargained. "Anything you tell us would be used for your benefit, we're here to help you," said Detective Smith. "All I know is that he shot me because he claimed me to be a traitor. I fled from my country with the help of a Jewish man."

"Fled, why did you flee then?"

"I ran away from my abusive husband and collided with the Israeli authorities. I received help from a friend and that's it."

"Who is this friend? What's his name?"

"I don't want to drag him into this. He's gone with his life and has nothing to do with me anymore."

"Joseph Weisman, a New York big shot lawyer. His face filled the press. He was with you throughout this whole process. He's way beyond dragged, he's the head of your issue." My eyes opened wide when he mentioned a big shot lawyer. I wondered why he said that. I have taken Joseph for a humble character. Big shot implied being famous, arrogant, and a jerk. Joseph did not portray those characteristics to me at all. "Well, you seem to know everything, so why are you questioning me anyway. I'm really tired and need to just get a break from this chaotic life I'm in," I said.

"Unless you're charging me with anything, I would appreciate it if you would leave me alone please, sir."

"I told you that what happened to you was a felony, the government can't just act like it didn't happen and forget about it," he snapped as he stood up. "Your situation may be more serious than you think. I'm trying to help you. You would also need to testify in open court against the defendant. Things could turn against you if you don't clarify your statement with me first. I have been assigned to help you." He put his notepad away in his inner pocket and headed out the door. "I'll see you later, hopefully and for your own sake, you would talk to me." He exited along with his partner unwillingly. Detective Harrison came back again and gave me his business card. "When you're feeling okay, give me a call," he said. "If I were you I would turn on the television." He marched out dissatisfied.

I used to always read the daily news off the Internet. I would not miss any issue, but when I became an issue, I could not reach it. In Palestine, I had no time. In Israel, I didn't understand the language spoken. In America, I'm afraid I won't be able to handle what was being spoken about me. I have always been friendly to society, but I doubted society's friendliness toward me. I ran my nurse's red button. A huge muscular man appeared at the door. "Do you need anything?" He startled me as he stood by the doorway, blocking the entrance. "I called for my nurse. Who are you?" I asked.

"I'm Tom, I'll be taking care of you while you're staying here," he said as he took a few steps forward. He stood like a solid metal bar. "What do you need?" he insisted. "Where's my nurse and who put you in charge of me?"

"Just tell me what you need," he took a few more steps forward. He started to intimidate me. "I need to put on the TV and I need the remote, please," I said, giving in like a child. Obviously, he had orders to follow. My orders were granted, but not the answers to my questions. I thought since he seemed harmless, I could live with that. Last thing I needed was an angry bodybuilder on my list. I felt uneasy and very misinformed as usual. If I had been a loud and tough-looking woman, people would not step all over me, even those trying to help me. He reached for the TV on the stretcher and moved it close to me. He had a solid facial expression. I couldn't read the writing on his face, but he represented an example of strength. He adjusted the TV and handed me the remote control. I wouldn't turn it on until he left the room, just for spite. I flipped the channels and stopped at the news channel. I witnessed my picture and name as the top issue being discussed by the public. Like a dissection of my character in the media, with amateur and reckless surgeons tearing me apart. The news reporter that conducted the story had no idea who I was. I wondered why she would mishandle my reputation. "Do you think that it was a love affair or a political conspiracy?" The reporter had the nerve to ask that question on air to a unanimous caller. "They were both involved in this whole thing from the beginning. I saw how he cried as she was rushed to the hospital. He completely dis acknowledged the camera crew surrounding them after the shooting of Salwa Adam. Mr. Weisman is a well-known man."

"I was among the passengers on the airplane, and the two seemed like a couple to me."

"What?" I shouted as the pain in my abdomen took a stronger effect.

"It can't be a love affair, that would be insane, I mean, a Muslim and a Jew, that's absurd and unethical," said the female reporter. "Joseph Weisman has a lot to lose, unlike Salwa Adam who no one really knows who she is," said the accompanying male reporter.

"Oh my god, where do I go after this? How do I live?" I said to myself at the same time the bodyguard came marching in. I wanted to cry from the painful words on the news and ignore the pain from the bullet. I looked at the bodyguard, horrified and with wonder. I needed to talk to someone who could tell me everything and make it sound nice.

"Are you okay?" he asked.

"Never been okay, I wish I had died from that bullet and not see the day where I am the center of media attention."

"Do you need me to put away the TV?"

"Yeah, that would just make it all go away," I said sarcastically and broke into tears. My echocardiogram machine went up. A nurse came rushing in as my heart rate went skyrocketing. She turned off the TV and pushed it away. "Why did you give it to her? We put it far away from her for a purpose," she said, charging Tom.

"My job is to take care of her needs and life. She asked me to turn it on. I had no idea it would upset her to that extent."

"Tell me, what else is being said? Leave the TV on! I need to know what is happening to me." I tried to push the nurse away as she was taking my pulse.

"You cannot afford to get upset, it is very bad for your wound," she said. Tom stood close, waiting to be told to do something, like a robot.

All I owned were my tears. I had my heart taken away from me when my father married me off to his nephew against my will. I lost my mind when I ran away from Palestine. I became practically disowned by the very people who owned me. My body was punctured like a wounded soldier in one woman's battle. I didn't know if I would end up in my home or an institute of some sort. Even my words were not heard. I had no chance of overcoming that plague that wrecked my being. How could they say whatever came to their mind on the news channels? Didn't they know that more harm would be attributed? The accusation of being a spy, and fear of escaping Israel did not hurt or affect me as deep as the accusation of the love affair. To top it off, how they ridiculed such an idea! Few days passed and I hadn't heard from Joseph or my family. I wondered why I wasn't given a phone. Completely disconnected from society, I have to admit I started feeling better. With Tom and the hospital staff my only companions, I felt safe for once in my life. I was able to get out of my bed and walk in the hospital hallway, close to my private room. Tom guarded me like a watchdog. I was given a pink flowered out-of-the-hospital pajamas. With no questions answered, I wore it. It felt good to receive compliments from the nurses. I healed well and wondered when I will be released. My new friends were a forty-year-old African American nurse named Sharon and Hannah, a twenty-seven-year-old young American nurse. Sharon had the night shift while Hannah cared for me during the day. I walked over to the large glass window behind Sharon's desk. I wanted to get a view of the city and the gleaming lights that peeked into the hospital. Sharon permitted me to walk on my own. I saw the people outside on the streets, waiting for something to happen. The flickering light aimed at me startled me; I covered my eyes and almost fell backward, had Tom not run to catch me. I couldn't believe that reporters and camera crews bunked outside the hospital in the dark, waiting to take a shot at me. "Maybe you should go lie down on your bed, Salwa," said Sharon as she gave Tom the signal to help me to my bed.

"I'm sick and tired of hiding and doing nothing," I said, stopping them from dragging me to my room. "What did I do that deserves that much judgment?"

"exceptional people like you are what the public craves," Sharon said with a friendly smile. I liked what she had said even though it had to be a lie.

"I'm amazingly miserable!" I added. "She's right, you may be stubborn, but you are amazing," commented Tom. His opinion backed Sharon's. A new side of Tom I hadn't seen before. With all those people outside the hospital, I feared being discharged. I lacked the energy and strength to deal with the unfair world. I went to my bed and tucked myself away from the press. It upset me being restricted from watching the news and being the only news followed and watched by others. I tried to understand why Joseph had kept away. I wished I could speak with him. He knew the right thing to say to my heart. I needed a computer or a laptop to do a little research of my own on Joseph Weisman. I got off my bed and walked over to Sharon's desk. Tom stood up and was angered by my fast return. "Didn't we agree that you need to stay in your bed and get some rest?" he said as if I made his job harder. I ignored him and kept making my way to Sharon. "Can I use your computer for a minute please?" I said calmly, hoping she would allow me.

"Why? Besides, I'm not allowed to let patients use the hospital's computer," she said.

"As a friend, please!" I pleaded. "Only for ten minutes, if I get caught, it may cost me my job," she said, looking around.

"Thank you, if anyone passes by, I'll just turn around to the window," I assured her. I eagerly went to Google and wrote down Joseph Weisman. I turned around and noticed Tom looking over my shoulder.

"A little privacy please. Do you need to guard my eyes too?" I said as I shut off the page. I gave him a moment to walk away. I resumed my research about Joseph. My face lit up when I came across his photograph under his name. I read the first page of researched information and viewed the most recent updates. My heart broke when I read the condolences sent to him from regarding his wife's death. I felt sad and ashamed for not knowing before. That explained his disappearance; the mourning of his wife's death was a legitimate reason. I wanted to add my condolences and send it to him. Tom apparently didn't leave me alone. I didn't notice him the second time, looking over my shoulders like an owl. He stopped me. "No, don't do that!"

"What is your problem? Who are you anyway?"

"You're going to have to trust me, and sending Joseph an email would harm you and him," Tom warned me. I shut off my research site in displeasure. I brushed by Tom with my head turned away from him. I didn't know to whom he would report my actions in searching for Joseph. Sharon followed me to my room. She caught me soaked in despair. I felt bad for Joseph, and I missed him even more.

"Don't worry baby. Someday, I just know it, you are going to have your dreams come true," she said, winking. She said what no one dared to say before. We both knew what she implied. I felt slightly comforted by her hopeful hint. I couldn't understand Tom; he refused to give me peace of mind and a good explanation either. After I stopped being in a grump, a small smile broke on my face when I remembered the photograph of Joseph. He couldn't have looked more handsome. I thought a movie star or a professional model would probably envy that pose he struck. I resented Tom for disturbing my research; I still didn't get enough information and knowledge about Joseph. I wanted to know everything that the public already knew, at least. Why were there so many secrets? Confusion filled up my mind. I felt spooked as I remembered my soon to be ex-husband. I feared my father might try to bring him to America just to book me forever. As far as he was concerned, I deserved what Sammy used to do to me. After all that has happened, I probably deserved more punishment. When would they ever leave me alone? I just needed to think things through and expand on my analysis of Joseph. He was guilty for being publicly favored. I would go down in a flash. If words couldn't hurt me, actions were going to kill me.

I rose from my bed and prepared myself for doom. My father and my brother informed the hospital they would be discharging me from the facility. With no place to go, I acted in acceptance with the whole idea. My father demanded my release. I had no predictions of my future. "I don't know what to do with you, and I can't believe what you put me through," he said. I ignored him; that was something I was really good at. The hospital staff monitored my reactions upon leaving. I had to portray that I approved of my father and smiled away the pain. Sharon gave me a good-bye hug. Hannah helped me comb my long hair. She gave me contact information if I felt any pain. She gave me her cell phone number and insisted I give her a personal call if I felt my life was in danger. I thought she stepped out of her professionalism by doing that, but it took a lot of courage and care for her to cross that line. Tom seemed stuck to me and tailgated us as we proceeded out of the room. My father hated Tom's presence around me. He hated any man that came close to me, even if crossing the street. "I got her from here," my father said, trying to get rid of Tom upon leaving. "He's a cop!" I whispered to my father. I lied just to avoid any fighting and to scare him away. If only he knew that I didn't even know where Tom came from or who put him in charge. "So what if he's a cop, that doesn't mean he can come home with us," my big brother shouted. I kept walking through the hallway and waved good-bye to the familiar nurses. Hannah held my arm and headed to the elevator. Tom came and held my other arm. My father pushed him away and took it. Tom held his fist to punch my father in his face. I screamed, "No, Tom, please, no!" Tom took a deep and long breath; he tightened his fist in the air and put it down slowly. My eyes did not let go of his until he completely backed off. "It is my job to help her, not marry her," Tom said to my father and brother in defense. "Tom, I'm okay, and thank you, really," I said, convincing Tom. Although I felt like I needed convincing. Hannah stood by the elevator in tears and gave me another long hug. "Take care of yourself, you hear."I smiled at Hannah to comfort her. I turned around and walked into the elevator with my father and my brother. Tom held the elevator door with his two hands, aggressively breaking into it. He made it inside and rode with us. Being in the elevator, I felt like being driven down to hell. I had a lot to be afraid of. The worst feeling is the fear of the unknown; it disables its owner, I thought. It felt extraordinarily warm and uncomfortable to be with my two family members. Tom's loyalty came to an end as we reached the lobby. That's when his duty ended with me. I lost sight of him as he disappeared. My father took out a black head scarf and told me to put it on my head. He said he didn't want me to be exposed to the public eye. I wished he would give me a better color at least. I had no control over my actions. I felt like a prisoner making her way through death row to face execution. If only the world could hear the screaming of my heart. My brother refused to exit through the front door entrance of the hospital after noticing the suspicious crowd that awaited a glance of me. We walked back to the main lobby, and my father requested to leave from the back exit. With his loud voice in argument, he got his way as usual. They knew well how to hide me away from everyone and erase my existence. My brother went through the back door and bought the car to pick us up.

CHAPTER TEN

Here Goes Nowhere!

They loaded me into the car like a piece of meat. They had no concern for my sadness or health. They succeeded at escaping from the crowd unnoticed. We rode in killer silence. They were cautious not to threaten me. Maybe if they did, I would've had a reason to run for help or scream to the world to save me from them. I bit my lips in fear; I felt my heart's endless weeping. I looked out of the window in search of a face that might recognize me or maybe offer to help a dying soul. I searched mainly for Joseph. I needed a miracle to find him in the busy streets of New York. I felt captured with no way out. I didn't travel a lot. My father pasteurized me from outside air. I knew I would get punished for every breath I inhale outside his boundaries and control. My brother drove like a maniac. He crossed a few red lights. I wished that he would get pulled over by the cops. My father sat beside me in the passenger seat. He couldn't stay silent anymore. "Who is that man the world has been talking about?" he asked me with his eyes burning in fury. Without being prepared for an early confrontation, I had to stall the conversation.

"Who do you mean?" When I played dumb, that always impressed him. If I showed any sign of intelligence, then that would threaten his ego.

"That man lawyer!" my brother shouted as he stepped on the brakes without a warning. "The only way to fix all that damage you created is if you would go back to your husband," my father said as an offer. "The country is better for you than here before you make a bigger mess out of the family," my brother said and continued driving recklessly. I had nothing to say. I turned my face away from their faces and viewed the skies. I prayed to God to save me from them. My father became angry and held my chin with his firm hand.

"Why aren't you saying anything?" I cried and pulled my face away from his grip. I wiped my tears with the tips of the head scarf I wore. My hands and legs shook rapidly. I felt as if I sat on a glacier of ice, except for my high temperature. They never listened to my opinion; I refused to speak to them. I defeated the temptation to defend Joseph. I knew if they got me, he would be safe from their harm. They considered anyone who offered me a helping hand as a threat. My father's impatience revealed his true intentions. "I'm going to tie you in the boiler room till you die if you refuse to return to your husband."

"We can't afford to make another mistake, Father. I think we'll keep her home until my cousin's immigration papers come out. They can live in our basement," my brother suggested. I slowly unlocked my door and waited for the right moment to escape out of the car. I had no idea or plan as to where to run to. All I could think of was escaping. We drove by the road near the ocean. As the car drove slowly through the traffic, I opened the door and ran out. My brother stopped the car. He yelled out that he'll catch me. He left my father to guard their car. I ran toward the ocean in tears. I wanted to jump into it. I avoided my abdomen pain and helplessly came close to the edge. Just then, my brother caught me as the people watched. They noticed me being dragged and didn't do anything. They watched in horror, but none took any action. My brother's car blocked traffic. My brother held my arm tightly, nearly suffocating my blood circulation. He walked me to the car. "I'm calling the police," said a woman jogger. I doubted she even had a phone. My father drove the car closer to us to avoid any more traffic jams and kept away from getting more attention. A black van pulled over next to my brother's car. A group of four masked and armed men came out and surrounded the area. My brother instantly loosened his grip on my arm. It became obvious they targeted me when one of them carried me quickly into the van. The rest of the men kept an eye on my father and brother. The driver in the van jumped to the opposite side of traffic and joined with the opposite side of traffic. The driver drove furiously and zigzagged through other vehicles. I felt like they drove me into a new dimension. They cheered out of excitement and gave each other high fives for a mission accomplished. They shared an excitement I couldn't define. I didn't know how I fell asleep and for how long.

CHAPTER ELEVEN

Kidnapped

I woke up in a small room alone. I took off the large bedcover on me. I looked around the room for details and clues. The room only had one square window with closed metal bars. I stood up and the pain from my wound throbbed. I walked around in the new room. I passed by the dresser with a mirror and nearly fell to the floor when I noticed myself in the mirror. I leaned against walls. I noticed two doors in that room, one completely shut while the other appeared half-open. I walked to it and noticed a small clean bathroom. I decided to wash my face with water and soap from the pump bottle. I fixed my hair with the brush by the sink. I felt too curious to weep for my condition. After I finished using the bathroom, I walked to the other door and tried to open it. Locked shut, I gave up my pursuit to open it. I couldn't guess where in the world I have landed. I felt well provided for. A small TV and a notebook laptop caught my eyes on a small desk on the other side of the bed. I felt glad and hoped they functioned. I leaped toward the two sets. I immediately turned the TV on and the light shined on my face off the TV set.

"Yes, it works!" I said to myself. Then I reached for the laptop and opened it up; my eyes opened wider when the power came on. I felt content and well fed. I had the two most important things that led to the outside world. It almost seemed like a joke. "Are they kidding me? What kind of kidnapping is this?" I said louder than before. I put down the laptop gently on the comfortable bed and sat on the small chair by the TV. I needed to watch the news, any kind of channel. I couldn't believe that I actually had cable, so I flipped the channels to CNN and then to the local news, back and forth. I stopped at CNN. I felt my life exposed by a special program. I finally got to see what has been said about me. They had to mention the kidnapping, I thought. Hopefully, I will become informed. The world knew more than I did regarding my state. My heart stopped when I noticed Joseph's picture behind the reporter. I reached for the volume button and nervously increased it. It seemed I jumped in too late, but not too little. Joseph gave a public speech in which a clip of it I captured. "Ms. Salwa Adam is not my love! My wife just passed away and I am still grieving her death. My children need my full attention and care at the moment. Therefore, we would appreciate it if the press stopped harassing us," he said with tears in his eyes. "I'm so dumb and I must've gone crazy to think that such a man would admit in public his compassion for me. I'm such a loser!" I cried and screamed hysterically. I threw myself to the bed and cried into the pillow as loud as I could hear. I faced a moment of insanity and despair. I refrained from crying with the sound of keys from behind the door. I lifted my head up in silence. It seemed like a large man behind the door. My eyes were blurry from crying; I blinked a few times and noticed a surprise guest. "Tom!" I said, surprised. He walked with a tray of food and water; he pushed the door with his leg and locked us both up with the key. He made his way to the dresser and put the tray down; he invited me to eat. "You must be starving, I bought you all vegan food," he said casually. "You, what is the meaning of all this, and when are you going to start explaining things to me?" I said in frustration. "You kidnapped me?"

"No, I helped kidnap you, you don't have to thank me," he said smoothly. He carried the food tray over to me and left it on my bed. He went and took the small chair. "How do you find this funny?"

"Just relax and eat your food. Maybe if you act like a good girl, I'll talk to you afterward. I might even answer a few questions."

"What exactly is going on, please answer me," I said, hoping to sound patient. "Eat first, talk later," he said, smiling. "Who made you my nanny?"

"Sarcasm won't work for you, now eat and shut up!"

"Who cares if I starve and die? I don't even care about me anymore," I said and stopped myself from crying. "I hate everyone and everything." I broke into tears and stuffed my face with the pillow again. I felt like a rebel with a million causes. Tom and I both listened to the news reporter when my name came up. "There are many suspects in Salwa Adam's kidnapping," said the reporter. She made me sound more serious than I thought. Tom watched my reaction; he kept the TV on to my surprise. "Aren't you afraid that your name would come up?" I asked, hoping to give him a scare. "I'm the last one they would suspect, I was your bodyguard," he said innocently. "But why did you do it? What are you going to get out of it? Ransom money? Fat chance, killing me would be easier for my family."

"You should stop talking and stop bothering me and yourself," he said and turned his face to watch the news. He ignored me. I liked being ignored; therefore, I started analyzing the food in front of me. I took a bite out of a slice of pizza. I longed for pizza ever since I was in Palestine. No one did pizza better than the Italians, I thought. The french fries smelled very fresh and fattening. "The novel she self-published may reflect on the relationship she had with Joseph Weisman," the TV reporter said. I coughed and nearly choked when I heard the news. Tom ran to me, patting on my back. He knew better than to pump my stomach that would've just killed me. I still needed an awful lot of healing to do, only time could manage. My dramatic life made it impossible to survive. "Did she just say I published the love story novel?" I said, trying to believe I didn't hear it alone."Well, did you write a novel or not?" Tom asked."I gave it to Joseph on the airplane from Israel," I said as my face transformed with a big smile. "He did care about me," I said, avoiding Tom and attending to the TV. Tom smiled for the first time and insisted I eat again. He took back his seat and crossed his arms while watching the news. My heart lit with happiness and my worries evaporated like passing clouds. I ate my two slices of pizza and greasy fries. I finished with a big gulp from the water bottle. After I finished eating, Tom looked at my tray. He stood up to carry away the empty tray. "Is there anything you need me to get for you?" he asked, picking up the tray."Are you leaving? You still didn't tell me why and who is behind all this, please," I said, holding on to his shirt."You'll know everything in due time, right now you're safe. No one can harm you, you're well protected. That's all I can say!" he said and loosened away from my grip. He feared saying any more. I followed him to the door. "You must rest in order to recover from the bullet wound," he said, pushing me back slowly. He left me alone with the TV. I turned around and remembered what I heard about my novel being published. I thought about how fast and sharp Joseph had been. He didn't waste one minute; he put my story to work. I worried about the new public accusations. I wrote that story way before I knew Joseph existed. I had no way of proving it. How sweet must he have been to work behind my back and take that risk. He may have done more had it not been for his wife's death. What would my father think after seeing my published story? If he didn't try to kill me, many others would. It would be impossible trying to get restraining orders for a million. While the news was on, I opened the laptop and sat on the bed. I looked up my name, why not? I thought. It overwhelmed me to see many articles already written about me and not one quote from me. How can the public trust that information? I wondered. I went straight to my new book publication. It stunned me to notice the number of books sold electronically and how the people are dying to get their hands on. Although the Jewish community opposed it and disliked it, they read it anyway. Controversy over it seemed terminal. I never imagined I would die from a world of threats and disapproval. A familiar speaker captured my attention to the TV screen, Detective Harrison's voice. "I'm going to find her and put those who kidnapped her in jail personally," he said with his face covering the screen. "Anyone who knows anything must contact the police immediately. I believe that her life might be in danger. We need to help send her home."

"No, don't do that," I said as if he could hear me. Every time I recalled being married, I felt the creeps. I hoped my father didn't help bring Sammy from overseas like he threatened before. I returned my focus to the Internet. I felt loved by one person in the world, Joseph, and that was more than enough for me. No wonder he said what he said on TV: that we didn't have a love affair. I began to understand why he had to say that comment. I went into searching for his history. He came from a different galaxy than mine. A very well-accomplished professional lawyer. He actually represented famous superstars and got off with millions in earned compensation. His reputation sounded very impressive. He received awards for being a prestigious attorney. He was big all right, but a bigger hero than I imagined. No wonder all eyes were on him. I, on the other hand, felt like a peasant compared to his status. I began to realize why he published my book that fast. For one thing, he really did have a brand name in business and his work received high respect even from politicians. Another reason he wanted to put me on top quickly for his own sake, I thought. He brought me up very fast and that made me noticeable. I guessed he had a head start on our secret project of peace. Hate came easier than love. Love required time and effort, hate destroyed things, I always believed. Those that hated me wouldn't stop at anything to banish me. While the ones who portrayed love made a difference in my life. I began to think that the kidnapping may have been the best thing for me at that time. Two weeks in solitary confinement, I began to show progress in my health and mental state. Tom became my only visitor. Picking on him made me feel tough. He became like an obnoxious big brother, yet contributed no harm. I looked forward to his arrival and what he bought for me every time he visited. I had no problem with being aloof; my reputation and my name had no aloof time. It disgusted me to follow the reaction of the merciless press. I watched with my hand on the chair and kept touring the room with my eye in constant horror the opinions of many of those who came close to even say hello to me. "Where did they find these people? Gibberish is all they knew about me. I never got close to anyone," I said to Tom one day at dinnertime visit. "The funniest thing was the dollar-store Chinese lady, she didn't speak English well enough to be interviewed, "Yeah, she comes over here sometime I see her,"Tom mocked and we both laughed. "I'm so ashamed, the world knows I'm poor!" I said, laughing harder. "Not for long," Tom said seriously. "Why do I always feel like I can't get anything out of you? What do you mean?"

"Okay, now knock it off and don't ask me any questions."

"That's not fair at all, you're like a thief that goes back to the people he robbed and returns some of the things he'd stolen from them. If you think I'm in this mess because of publicity, then you're dead wrong," I said.

"Okay, for one thing that book that's circulating the world, didn't you expect for one minute that maybe you'll earn a few dollars at least or what?" he said, heading out the door. I thought for a moment and realized that it didn't occur to me."I'm sorry, you didn't have to get so upset. Wait, I need to ask you a favor," I said manipulatively. "What's the other thing that's going to make me not poor?"

"Good night for now," he said, stepping out the door. "Oh, wait, that's not the favor, I really need some fresh air, how about a walk in the park or a visit to the library, whatever I don't care. I just need to see the sunlight for God's sake. You're making me feel like you're my daddy and prison guard," I said.

"Okay, I'll see what I can do tomorrow, good night," Tom said, shutting the door behind him and locking it with the key. I wondered all night what Tom might have meant by "not for long." He knew too much, and I needed to analyze every word he said. He seemed very well coached. I felt challenged to crack into his mind. He kept everything between us strictly business and humble. The only time he got personal was when his girlfriend called him on his cell phone. Well, he didn't get personal with me. I just heard him tell her not to worry and that everything would be fine. It seemed like she had a problem that he refused to share. The interesting thing was that he closed the conversation with her, saying, "Okay, boss."

"That was not his girlfriend at all, it was definitely his boss. How did I miss that?" I said, scratching my head in deep thinking. Every time he pretended to be speaking with his girlfriend, it was actually the big boss behind my kidnapping for sure, I felt glad by my new findings. I hoped to use it to my advantage next time I met Tom. Watching too much news made me sick and I felt ready to defend myself. The more I stayed away, the stronger I felt, and the more lies were being spread. I went from runaway to spy to love affair. I feared what might oppress me next. Tom skipped breakfast for me. I wondered if I had really upset him. I thought that inside that big man lived a big baby. By noon, he came. I didn't stand up to greet him as usual. I kept my nose in the laptop. "Honey, I'm home," he said, which forced me to smile. "Am I being punished? You skipped breakfast on me and no lunch. To whom shall I complain about you, sir?" I said, looking at the shopping bag he held in his hand. He threw it at the bed and said, "Put those on, your wish has been granted."

"What? Am I leaving this place? To where?"

"You are permitted to step out for a break," he said, unpacking the bag. I snatched the bag open. It contained a large pair of black shades. A New York Yankees cap. A short blond wig. The sky blue top impressed me. It was a very long shirt with a white belt around the waist. A light blue pair of jeans screamed my name. Original and not my style, I planned to wear them anyway. I carried all the material in my arms as I went to the bathroom to change. Tom lay in bed to rest for the first time. He appeared tired yet proud of his purchase. He crossed his legs and put one arm on his forehead while watching the TV. "If my father could see me now, he won't recognize me," I said, stepping out of the bathroom while fixing the wig on. Tom sat up in astonishment. "I don't even recognize you, and I saw you a few minutes ago." He crossed over to me and asked, "Are you ready for this? You won't try to run away, will you?"

"Now where would I go? Trust me like I trust you," I said, putting on my humongous shades. "Seriously, couldn't you find a bigger pair?"

"What did you expect, reading glasses?" We headed toward the door. Tom's phone rang, and he stepped back into the room to take the call. I waited against the door impatiently. I feared that we would never get out of that room. I needed to see civilization. I missed the smell of the streets filled with the gas pollution coming out of cars. I wanted to see my friends, the birds, and the pigeons. My eyes longed to get a big look at the passing clouds in the deep skies. Nature, to me, was where peace existed. Human beings, on the other hand, disturbed that peace. I appreciated every tree I saw. To me, they were also living things with hidden emotions. Tom walked to the end of the room before speaking on his phone. That caused me to be suspicious. It had to be his boss. "Tell your girlfriend I said hello," I mocked. He lifted his eyebrows at me. He shut me up by waving his hand in the air. It appeared that he was engaged in a risky conversation. I stopped myself from joking and speaking. I hated to lose my privilege of leaving that room. I walked over to the mirror and smiled at my appearance. My new American look disguised the Arabic Muslim woman in me. I had difficulty concealing my long black hair under that small wig. The blue cap helped keep my hair intact. I didn't understand why I had to wear a wig and a cap together. I felt glad he didn't get me a scarf. "I can't do that!" Tom's voice became louder on his phone. I turned to him and wiped my smile away. "I have the guys guarding from a distance. It's not that big of a deal," Tom lowered his voice again. "We've been through this already. I promised and I can't back down from that," he said as he turned and faced me. I put my hand on my heart in worry. It seemed that the boss had second thoughts about me stepping out. "I'm doing it anyway." Tom slammed the cell phone. Without any hesitation, he unlocked the door angrily and said, "Let's get the hell out of here." He fought for me in a way that a brother would. I liked his disobedience to his boss. He seemed to carry me out with responsibility and loyalty. He held his posture and walked me out the door as his eyes did the guarding from side to side.

CHAPTER TWELVE

The Park

Like a nature-deprived animal, I wandered through the city's park. Tom cut me loose and made me roam in freedom. My pleasure was his distress. He watched me from a close distance. He watched with caution anyone else who came near me. I felt like the president's daughter, being looked after by scattered chaperones. I drank my freshly squeezed berry fruit smoothie slowly. I enjoyed every step I took and appreciated every sip I drank. The park seemed crowded more than usual. I thought it was because of the perfect weather. The breezy winds and the sunshine attracted the population to walk, jog, or run in that park. I looked at a couple sitting by the benches and tested my new look. They didn't recognize me at all. I felt excited when I noticed a middle-aged woman holding my novel and reading it. I walked over to her. "Excuse me, what is that you're reading?"

"It's the new best seller novel. It's very controversial, so I wanted to see for myself."

"Can I take a small look at it, if you don't mind?" I said, Tom interrupted, "I mind!" He said and pulled me away. "One important rule, no associating with anyone, do you want to get us both in trouble?"

"It's not like she knew me or I was asking her for help," I said, walking away from Tom annoyed.

"I sacrificed a lot to get you out for a while, don't screw it up," Tom said, trying to catch up with me. I walked ahead of Tom and he followed. I looked around for the loud barking of dogs. Tom looked around curiously. He drew me closer to him as we viewed two large k-9 dogs from a distance, heading our direction. They were being held by two police officers. "I'm scared of dogs, especially if they are chasing and barking at me," I said nervously. "Walk casually, don't be scared, they can smell your fear, not your name," Tom said, encouraging me to pick up my pace and change into a different direction. "They are not chasing you. It's just your fear is making you paranoid."

"Paranoid? They're catching up with us, and you call me paranoid," I said, looking back. "Stop you two, over there!" the officers called. They picked up their speed from the leashed dogs. They were unable to control the ropes and ran as well as the dogs. "Okay, stop, if they get suspicious, I want you to run to the van, without looking back," Tom whispered. I felt tense and unstable. Tom took out his cell phone and whispered in it, "Get the van ready and look out."

"We're looking for a young female, a Muslim Palestinian, she was kidnapped about two weeks ago. The search for her has driven the city's officials mad," said the officer. "How can we help?" Tom stood still and appeared calm. The dogs frightened me and I couldn't remain calm. "Please keep your dogs away, I'm afraid of dogs," I said, trying to escape. Tom held me tight and stopped me. "Do you mind taking off your shades, miss?" I felt a sense of being in trouble. The black van came driving furiously on the grass toward us. I turned around quickly, which caused my hair to fall out of the small wig and cap. I dropped the cold drink in my hands to the ground. The policemen let go of their dogs. Tom stood in front of me and yelled, "Jump in the van, go!" He wrestled with the charging dogs. I screamed and looked at the van. I didn't know if I should go inside the van or go with the cops. I felt confused as I looked at Tom pushing the dogs away. The cops withdrew their weapons and pointed them at Tom and me. The van opened the passenger seat and a man called out, "Get in!" I looked at the cops, at Tom pushing away the dogs, and then at the van. A man stepped half of his body out of the van, snatched me, and forced me inside the vehicle. I screamed out loud because of the pressure that he squeezed on my surgery wound. My wound ached; the van took off like a wild horse. Tom couldn't follow, but fell to the ground by a bullet or from the dog that took him down. I cried and screamed for Tom. I felt devastated for him. I heard another shot fired at the van. The driver missed the bullet that targeted his wheels and kept driving. I looked through the window glass at Tom as I rode off with my new escapees. The police officers handcuffed his hands behind him. I noticed the police officers retrieved their fire because of the panic caused by the pedestrians. I heard police sirens from a distance, but the driver paid no attention to it. I closed my eyes in agony of the pain in my abdomen. Two men captured me in a black van. One drove while the other attended to me. I felt horrible, being in the middle of all that trouble. Within minutes, we were out of sight of the police. I felt like I was drowning deeper and deeper into the hollow sea of confusion. I covered my grief into my palms and exploded in crying for my misfortune. Earth seemed small for me to handle and exist on it. With a sense of despair and disappointment, I halted my tears. I thought that no good could come from crying. I suddenly became numb. The driver stopped the van. The man who sat beside me told me it's time to leave that van. "What now?" I asked. "Get off, this is your stop," he said. Every time I remembered Tom, I felt more hopeless. Those muscular men reminded me of him. I didn't expect to care about him the way I did. I guessed because he did care about my wound, it had to come back to him somehow. They unloaded me out of the black van and shoved me into a different white Jeep. I watched them drive away from the white van. They disappeared like a flash of lightning. I had my hands on my belly and my head bent down. I didn't look at the new vehicle's occupants. I hoped that the cops noticed that I fled by force from the park's scene. They didn't have anything on me. I felt almost sure that the surveillance cameras in the park would reveal the truth. My head remained down until I heard someone say, "Hello there, my Arabian princess." I lifted my head in curiosity and my mouth dropped open when I noticed Joseph.

"What? Don't tell me that you're?" I said and stretched my eyes wider. I wanted to double-check that it really was Joseph who sat next to me in the backseat of the vehicle. "I wouldn't call me boss, but it sounds good coming from you," he said smiling. His smile turned into a frown when he noticed my tears on my face. My two hands held my stomach from the pain. His face filled with worry, and he lost that boss appeal. "Why are you aching? Who hurt you?"

"What difference does it make?"

"Let me take a look at it," he said, trying to touch my stomach. "I thought you're a lawyer, not a doctor," I said, refusing his gesture. "Why are you mad at me? What I did was for your own good."

"Mine or your status?" I said, looking away. "Are you going racist on me?" he said as he captured my smile. I had no idea what to do. I threw my head back at the seat. My pain made it harder to carry on an argument with Joseph. I felt a weakness in my legs and felt wetness from the blood on my shirt. I lifted my hands off and Joseph and I became astonished by the bloodstains. "You're bleeding again, how did that happen?" he said horrified. He opened his phone and dialed a number. "You idiot, I told you to carry her into the van, not crush her," Joseph shouted through the phone and shut it fast. He insisted on looking at my wound. I lifted my shirt and noticed that blood came from between the staples on the wound. His hand became soaked in my blood. "Tom got shot, he'll probably tell you now," I said, looking for Joseph's reaction.

"I need to get you to a hospital, you're bleeding," he said. "No, wait, what am I going to say to them, and what about Tom?"

"Don't worry about Tom, worry about yourself!" he said angrily. I covered my stomach with my shirt to get his attention. "Drive to the hospital!" Joseph called out to the driver of our automobile. "No! I'm not going until you explain to me what the hell just happened and what are we going to do about this big jumble we're in."

"After you take care of that," he said and pointed to my belly. "I'm sorry things turned out this awful. I didn't mean to bring you any grief," he said in dismay. "It's nothing severe, just a little blood, "I said calmly and I avoided the show of discomfort. "This world is not big enough for you and me together." He frowned in disagreement to my statement. "It's a puddle, and you're going to see someone for it. Keep driving to the nearest hospital." He patted the driver on the shoulder to proceed with the order. I looked at him in wonder and amazement. I looked at him in a new perspective yet better. As scrambled as things got, he continued his involvement in my business. He could read my mind like no other psychic. Even if I tried to make him upset and push him away, he saw right through me. He made it hard to detach from him. "I need to ask you a million questions, but just answer me one for now. Why kidnap me?"

"I needed to protect you from many people. I thought if you're away and out of people's eyes, you would heal and be safe. When you earned the public's affection, then everyone would help protect you," he said as he fixed my hair off my face. "What a heroic stunt. Is that what all that was?" I sat upward.

"No! The gunman was released on bail the same day of your hospital discharge. He threatened to get you anyway. According to him and some others, murder would be a heroic stunt. I couldn't sit and watch what happened to you. Trust me, I know that he would stop at nothing till your dead, or until he's behind bars for good. I'm going to stand against him in court. It's already official."

"You have jeopardized my chance of innocence through your irrational behavior."

"I did it for you, and I wanted you to stay away until he gets convicted. There would be over a hundred witnesses against him." He seemed upset and wanted some apology from me. I knew he meant well and wished that there could be any way to avoid going back to the hospital. We remained tangled with unresolved issues. I gave him my condolences on the passing away of his sick wife. I asked about the condition of his children and how they were handling things. If only time could freeze and allow us to divert in conversations. He reached for his pocket and gave me a new iphone. He urged me to use it only for private matters. I had no one to reach out to besides him. That was all I needed. He advised us to keep it away from any family members or police. With my hands on my pain, he reached for my jeans' side pocket and slipped the phone in. I watched him with fascination. "Consider it my gift to you," he said as his fingers nearly tickled me. "I didn't get you anything," I said. "Just take care of yourself, that's my gift from you. Remember, I'm always a phone call away. I won't call you, but you can call me anytime or send a direct message."

"Yes, captain!" I said, saluting him. He seemed too concerned to smile. We were pulled over by the hospital I have been admitted to previously. Joseph and I were silent for a moment. "What do you want me to do?" the driver asked. Joseph looked around and back at me. "I suggest you go in, they'll help you once you reach the emergency door," he said in a deep low-pitch tone. "Go before the security approaches and sees us together," he said as if that was what I wanted to hear. I felt frozen. There was so much I wanted to say to Joseph. I hated to disconnect from him. I ignored his suggestion. We were parked a couple of feet away from the entrance to the hospital's emergency room. His lips pressed together, I could see the tension of his jaws. "What do I say?" I asked him for guidance. "Say whatever makes you happy," he said, withdrawing himself backward. "You can tell them about me, Tom, anything. It's up to you. Just go and get help for that bleeding." He opened his door and came running around to my door. He unlocked my door and stretched out his hand to me. I looked at his fine waistline and then up at his sad facial expression. I loved the color black of clothing he wore. We escaped the risk of being recognized by anyone. I feared his exposure; therefore, I gave him my hand. He squeezed it tight and pulled me out gently towards his chest for a warm embrace where I can hear the silent weeping of his heart. He pulled me closer and tighter, stealing a hug from me and kissed my head. I tried to stand straight, but the pain hindered me. He pulled me upward. His open arm around me felt like a warm nest. He started to withdraw his hands slowly. I felt my heart breaking for him. His eyes were like a web of red veins. I held his hand tight again. I took one last dive in his green yet restless eyes in disclosure. He hung on as he walked me a few steps closer to the emergency room's entrance. An ambulance man and woman came running to us after they noticed the blood on the ground. They approached in panic. I slid my hand from Joseph's warm palm. "Please go, I'll take it from here!" I said, reminding him to take cover. His eyes seemed like a pool of water that he controlled from splashing on his face. I headed toward the door with the help of the ambulance attendants. "We need a wheelchair or a bed stretcher!" the woman said. She dressed as an ambulance operator. She pushed the door open. I took one last look behind me. I felt relief as I saw Joseph facing the direction of the car that carried us. Faced with external bleeding, I felt internal bleeding of my heart. I had blood everywhere, and I left a trace behind me. I received critical and private care from the hospital staff. I felt like being sent back to boot camp hospital. I remembered the same scent that still lingered in my nose a while ago. The alcohol smell mixed with medications. Slight warmth comforted me. I felt myself fade out and appear unconscious.

CHAPTER THIRTEEN

Hospital Return

There he stood, Detective Harrison, on my shoulders. He seemed astonished at my presence. I wondered how he arrived that quickly to where I settled in. I closed my eyes, hoping he didn't notice that I faked being asleep. I had to avoid his testimony. He roamed back and forth in my new private room. His partner stood quietly. "If only we could figure out who did this to her!" I heard Detective Harrison say. "Then we can end this entire charade." I hoped he would leave me alone. I had a lot on my mind that I didn't want to share with him. "Who brought her here to this hospital?" Mr. Harrison addressed the nurse that walked into the room. "I have no idea, you might ask the attendants who took care of her in the ER," the nurse replied as she approached me. I decided to open my eyes and look at the nurse as she changed my IV bag. "I see you still haven't changed much since last time we met," said Mr. Harrison. "It's nice to see you again, sir," I said and sat slightly upward. "Do you mind answering some old and new questions?" he asked. I waited until the nurse walked away and then shifted my attention to the two detectives. They stood side by side and had serious expressions on their face. Detective Harrison stood with one foot on the chair and the other on the ground. He faced me and demanded answers. "Who drove you here? Was it your kidnappers? That is if you were really kidnapped," he said with his shoulders leaning closer to me. "Are you questioning me or accusing me?" I said, crossing my arms. "What we need to know is who did this to you?" Detective Smith asked. He had a calmer and gentler tone than Harrison did. He made me feel less intimidated and seemed to be holding Harrison away. He stood closer to my bed. "I don't know who really is in charge. All I knew was a man named Tom. He helped hide away for a while. I'm sure you met him by now."

"We have him, and he said he planned the whole kidnapping on his own," said Mr. Smith. "I'm not buying that bologne story, we have statements from witnesses that saw four kidnappers, not one."

"Well, ask him, I don't know."

"Why do I feel like you're hiding a lot of things from us?" Detective Harrison asked. He gave me the impression that he knew more than I did. He pushed the chair with his foot and walked toward me. "One thing I need to know and I'll leave you alone, is Joseph Weisman part of this whole deal you're in?" I looked down and rested my hands on my wound. I meant to distract the two men from answering. I looked at the blood sac that was hung and attached to the needle in my vein. I had nowhere to run from the heat of their eyes. I faced them unhappily. "Why would he be? What does he contribute in care?"

"You didn't answer my question, yes or no!" Harrison said impatiently. "What are you trying to impose?" I asked. Detective Smith blocked Harrison and turned to me and said, "You see, Mr. Weisman might either be involved or in danger in this case." Harrison seemed impressed by how Smith got my calm attention and acceptance.

Mr. Smith hit on an intelligent queue. "Okay, another thing, you're going to have to testify against, the gunman who shot at you in the airplane," said Harrison. "He is set to go on trial next week. That could be the motive behind your kidnapping and your new added injury." I had forgotten all about the gunman despite the pain I felt which he inflicted on me. I looked at the IV of blood and wondered whose blood was injected into my system. Curiosity took over me. I had nothing to say, so I rested my back and slipped into the covers. "I want to go home," I said to Detective Smith. Harrison seemed irritated by my request. He walked to my other side of the bed. "There won't be a home for you if you don't work with me," he said, and Smith couldn't prevent him from getting closer. I wanted to go home because I knew my father's jealousy would keep all people away. I didn't feel like it was surrender, but a temporary hideout. "You get shot, then kidnapped, and now returned to the hospital bleeding and you want out." He stomped his foot on the floor and twirled his body away angrily. I never put them together that way. "Joseph Weisman," he said and turned around looking for my reaction. I felt stirred on the inside and hoped to appear stable. I looked at Detective Harrison and raised my eyebrows in question. "What are you saying?"

"Does that name mean anything to you?" he said and stood with his fist on his side, close to his gun. I couldn't help but feel angry. He pointed out that the new novel I had written must be about Joseph and me. I had no way of proving that it wasn't. I didn't have the energy to fight and explain myself, but I had to give it a try. He exclaimed that Joseph maybe the reason for my big disorderly situations. "I wrote that story back in Palestine when I had a few moments at a time of free time. It took me a year to arrange. I met Joseph about a month ago. There was absolutely no connection in between."

"Well, you both lived most of your lives in America and obtained American citizenship. We checked the time he had arrived in Israel the year before, and both of your names appeared on that same flight.

Both of you fled from Israel back to the US and again on the same flight. You want to convince me how all that just coincidence? I'm sure not. It looks more like an affair to me," he said with confidence and pride in his thesis. I despised his accusation and found myself sinking in deep thought. I started asking myself the same questions. I couldn't believe how all that could have been coincidence. I found myself lost, and everything I did was used against me. I felt I needed to write a book just explaining my new situation and misunderstandings. I felt a sense of relief when Sharon, my previous nurse, came strolling in the room and greeted me with a warm hug. "I couldn't believe it when I heard that you're back in here, so I came to check on you for myself," she said loudly. I hoped she would help me get rid of the two detectives. I admired her strength. "Are these men giving you a hard time?" she asked and turned around to analyze them. I nodded my head. "Excuse me, gentlemen, but you need to leave and give Ms. Adam time to rest."

Mr. Harrison seemed desperate for an answer and he wouldn't budge at Sharon's request. He persisted in his implications of Joseph and me. I thought he could even inform me more. "One thing, Detectives, I wasn't kidnapped and I won't press any charges against Tom. I'll say he was a bodyguard and wanted to protect me."

"Who appointed him as a bodyguard? Joseph, why?"

A good citizen and a fellow human friend," I said and I felt like I scored a goal. That made Harrison lose his temper. He rubbed his hair out of agony. "Since when was it a crime for someone to look after a friend?"

"Since national security and order are at stake," he said and put up his chest in great defense. Sharon decided to end the pressure in that room and guided the two men out. They were swept out by her attitude and her superior oud tone. "You will be seeing me again and again, I promise," said the detective. One thing I couldn't resist, I couldn't trust anyone and I needed to make the situation less than they were bound to escalate. I owed Joseph to keep his name and reputation clean and safe. I started to wonder if Joseph and I ever met before. I searched my memory bank. I thought harder and tried to remember the last time I traveled back to my country. I remember feeling like being drafted to an international army. My father's speech stood out loud in my mind, his threats against me vividly heard by surrounding waiting passengers. I wondered if Joseph had been around and heard everything at that time. Although it did make sense, I forced myself to remember that day. It hurt me recalling every word my father said. "You go back to your husband. The only way you'll ever leave him is if you die." I remembered thinking what if he did; did that mean I had to kill myself? I remember him cornering me and finishing his speech with a painful thrust. His body language distinctively portrayed a complex issue. He used extreme hand gestures; those who didn't hear him speak just watched and passed by. How could I have not expected my husband to abuse me when my father did the same? He chose me as a man that resembled him in action. His deep compassion for his nephew defeated my attempts of divorce. My husband got arrested by the Israeli police a year before we got married. He threw rocks at an Israeli vehicle in the streets of Ramallah in a rally. That made him like a hero who deserved a trophy wife in reward once released. He was unable to leave the country due to his criminal conviction. That exhausted the process of his immigration papers. I filed them right away and came to the US three months later. Since his papers didn't go through, my father took me to an immigration lawyer. I had to act like I really needed to bring Sammy to the US. The lawyer didn't put his heart in helping me because I didn't even believe in my case. My father seemed like a loyal man when he handed me over to his town and nephew for free. He bought my dowry and gave his nephew credit for purchasing it in public. My father's name and image in front of his tribal people rested on my cooperation. Being raised in America, I begged to differ and felt the challenge of an upcoming battle. Arranged and forced into a miserable marriage without any consideration to my feelings. I would not have minded if my husband turned out to be kind and sweet. Instead, his jealousy blinded him from treating me well. There were times I felt he was jealous of me, not for me. I finally remembered seeing Joseph at the airport; I smiled to myself and wanted to jump out of my bed. I remember my father and mother dropping me by the airplane's entrance gate. I didn't know why I cried even more after they turned away and left me alone. It wasn't that I like I was attached to them, but a feeling of anguish and doom. I remembered my shoulders brushing against a well-dressed man. We collided accidently upon going through the last checking desk for stamping. He did have Joseph's descriptions. I glanced for a quick and vague glance. He wore glasses and smelled fresh. He appeared as a handsome older man. I dropped my passport, which caused him to drop his passport also. I felt drowned in my tears and my vision seems cloudy. He picked up both passports. I hid my face in my napkin, waiting for him to figure out who's who. As my head faced down, he handed it to me. I pictured the shine of his wedding ring on his right hand index finger. He slipped away before I could thank him. By the time I looked up at him, he had walked way ahead of me. That must have been Joseph, without a doubt in my mind. Maybe Detective Harrison was right. What I wrote could have been inspired by that Jewish man at the airport, Joseph. I felt the inspiration to write a novel about a Palestinian woman and an Israeli man finding true love in one another. I had to find the means of coping and surviving. Writing helped me release my worries and fears on paper. Trust became extinct in my life with no one to confide in. I thought about that man throughout my flight. Once we got off the airplane, I searched for the well-dressed man. There were a few men dressed in suits. They were all Israelis. From a distance, I realized a man who had the same posture left ahead of me. In that huge crowd, my eyes couldn't follow. I engaged in a bigger distraction, the arrival of my husband and his mother. I felt grateful for Detective Harrison's insight that made me see things clearer. I also felt horrible that I didn't know Joseph knew me way before I knew him. I guessed that men are better at keeping secrets like they say. I felt the urge to contact Joseph and speak with him. I found no privacy with my family charging into the hospital to take me away. I thought it would make my father go easy on me if I called him to discharge me from the hospital. I needed to hand myself in, the consequences would be less harmful. He would cut me some slack, I hoped. I portrayed an extreme bad health state, which granted me some mercy upon leaving the hospital. My home lacked the sweetness like bitter coffee. I felt handcuffed by my father and brother and driven to an execution chair. I had to face judgment at home before I could win judgment out in the world and the wild. I hid the phone that I received from Joseph securely into my undergarment. I wrapped my heart and buried all the care I carried for Joseph. I had to be strong and conceal all my emotions under any circumstances. Joseph had become my only weakness and worry. Leaking that secret meant my eternal prison and possible death. I wished for no more negative surprises. I didn't inform Joseph of my discharge with my father. I knew that would trigger his worries about me. I feared he would interfere again and cause more uprising. He had to stay out of the picture in order for me to win a divorce battle. I had to fix that issue by myself. Back from the grave and buried into another. I felt strength within, although I appeared demolished. A secret smile accompanied me, knowing I can contact Joseph anytime I wanted. I felt his presence and care shine in my pathways. My sisters and brothers awaited my arrival at my home.

CHAPTER FOURTEEN

Home Sweet Home?

Harsh greetings from my family made me feel I have been a bad daughter and sister. I entered with pain and disappointment in the pain they caused me. They stood like a victimized army, I being the one soldier to blame their failures on. I approached my mother for a kiss and hug; she stiffened her back and paid no affection back. My oldest sister Nashwa occupied herself with her newborn baby girl. My younger sister carried herself in displeasure and stood by my mother. My brothers were steaming with anger and retaliation. They waited in a queue from my father. I guided myself to the single seat couch and sat gradually. I knew their eyes were fixed on me. I felt absolutely nothing for their abusive and oppressive stares. I knew I had done nothing deliberately wrong. I grew up with the rule that your actions are judged by your intentions. I craved a home-cooked meal. I smelled roast beef with onion and garlic. I hated that smell. Being a vegan made me nauseous from the spicy cooked beef essence. I felt that my punishment had started. They all knew how I felt about meat, especially red meat. I grew up in Palestine in a poor village. Meat was not introduced to me. By the time I grew up, I had no taste or desire for it. Worse than that, seeing it in abundance kills me. It didn't make sense to me to eat other animals' body parts. I did hope for some rice and salad. The only food I could never get sick of any time of the day or year. I felt it was too soon for me to walk into the kitchen and serve myself. It didn't look like I would receive any royal treatment any time soon. My nephews and nieces ran around in the large house. Everyone gathered yet engaged with one another. The outcast had begun. I looked at the TV and used the same treatment on them. I ignored them and cautiously kept to myself. I needed to set my eyes on something that spoke or seemed to speak to me. Very bad timing of my name appearing on TV, I thought. My big brother rushed to the screen and turned it off. His action resembled a child teasing for demanded attention. I remained subtle and patient. The last thing I needed was a breakdown of my nerves. My father sat across from me and everyone else sat around him. "Since when have you worked as a spy for the Israelis?" he asked and held my brother from asking another question. "When could I possibly have had the chance or time to see the Israelis, except on the day of coming to the US?" I said in defense. "Sammy wouldn't allow me outside the house at all. The Israelis were never invited to that house anyway." My brother seemed to stand up and close his fist. My father pulled him down and my older sister stopped him as well. I turned my head away from all of them and looked at the large open window. Windows always reminded me of hope and a small way out of tight places. My younger brother stood in front of it and blocked my sight.

"What about that Jewish man you were with? I swear to God I could just kill you right now," said my big brother. I felt glad they didn't say "kill Joseph."

"There is no way you can clean your name and our family's name again after you were seen with him," said my father. "There you said it, seen with him. Just like being seen with a bus driver on the bus or a policeman giving you a ticket. Or the store's clerk or the mailman. There is a big difference between seen with and actually—" My father raced to me and slapped my face before I finished my line. The room turned silent after the loud smack he struck me with.

My eyes filled with tears. I resisted letting them run down my face. I had no control over my trembling lips and the heat pounding on my left cheek. I almost heard a subliminal applause by the audience in front of me. My mother shrieked and returned to my father in support. I kept my head down and bit my lip to stop myself from arguing any further. I wished the earth would open up and swallow me. I wanted to be forgotten. "Your relatives in New York would be holding an Arab open court for you before they decide what should be done with you or that man you were with," my father said. He finalized the meeting with a bigger dread and problem. How dare they take me to a higher level for questioning? I wondered what they had in store for Joseph. They could easily have harmed him and make it look like an accident. I stood up and disregarded my sisters who blocked my way. I made it past them and went to my old bedroom. "You will be staying in the basement and not leave it till I say so," my father's voice followed me. I kept walking to my bedroom. Then I felt a pulling of my shirt and hair from the back. It was my big brother; he practically dragged me down the stairs mercilessly. He threw me in and shut the dark room and slammed shut the door behind him. I searched for the light switch and opened the light. I leaned against the wall and cried with my forehead pressed against it. I turned around and noticed my old belongings in a brown cardboard box next to the bed. I slowly dragged my aching heart to the pillow and cried as loud as I could without being heard. I lay on my bed and wandered the room with my eyes. The basement felt cold and lonely. It felt like a dungeon, and the short ceiling caved in on me. I took out my phone. I turned the power on and streamed for any new text messages from Joseph. The rule was that he is to text me only and I would be the one to ever call. When the power came on, there were about twenty messages in the inbox. I needed some comfort and understanding more than before. I smiled upon reading the new greetings from Joseph. He addressed me as an Arabian princess. If only he could see me then, I was anything but that. He insisted I reassure him of my health status and condition. The last message he seemed angry to find out I had left the hospital without informing him. He urged me to reply as soon as I could. I couldn't call him or send a text reply because of my irrational emotional state. I feared to send the wrong message that would make him panic and do something crazy. I read all his messages over and over. They felt like bandages to my wounded soul. I decided to send him a positive and upbeat note.

Not a moment too soon did I receive a reply from Joseph. It was as if he waited to hear from me. I felt guided and protected despite the distance. He replied with concern and fear. He didn't seem to buy my story, yet again, he let me get away with it. I sent him a last word and said that someone is coming down the stairs, and I needed to shut the phone quickly. I didn't realize that Joseph would know that I was alone and down some stairs. He would figure it out sooner or later. I planned to fix that message when I had the time. I put the phone under my pillow and sat up to view who was opening the door. My oldest sister Nashwa walked toward me with a suspicious stare. "What happened to you? You were never like that. You went and disgraced us like the way you did."

"What happened is that I died every day and no one even thought of getting me out. You're all like robots, programmed by Dad," I said to her. She seemed angry and thought hard of a reply and walked around looking for something to complain about. "It's that man everyone is talking about. He got you this far here and who knows what he'll do next," she said, taking a seat by the end corner of my bed. My younger sister walked in on us and engaged in the conversation. She obviously heard my other sister's comment and added, "Tell me about that guy, he's really handsome and sexy. Too bad he's Jewish and you're still married." I thought that they were shallow. They couldn't see beyond the cover of my situation. They both lacked understanding and depth. I knew that they were sent to interrogate me for my father. That's how it worked: you help him and then you get a merit of approval from his authority. It drove me crazy when I'm referred to as married. I didn't like it before and I hated it more at that time. I thought marriage depended on consent and acceptance from both parties. Only one spouse's consent should make a marriage invalid I perceived. "I can't believe that you two would think so unholy of me and assume that I would do anything against God," I said and rolled my eyes at them. I had no problem fighting them verbally. My older sister continued her suspicious gaze at me. "You must be hiding something. You seem happy about something. I can tell from the tiny little smile you work to conceal from us," she said. I had to admit she wasn't as shallow as I had thought. I guessed older age did come with a little more wisdom. An Arabic proverb says, "Older than you by one day knew more than you did by one year worth." How could they expect me to confess about something I didn't do? Or even trust their intentions and handling of my issues. They're blinded from the real truth and self-centered on their lives. They both accepted their arranged spouses and learned to love them. I had to be different and an outcast. That made me more of a rebel. Seeking a way out made me a criminal. The first person who came in my way of support, they wanted to get rid of by accusations. I felt convinced that Joseph happened to be at the right place and at the right time in my life. No one could accuse me enough to disengage in his unconditional support. There was nothing more to that. He represented a dear friend to me; maybe I was fond of his character and admired his actions. What made that forbidden? A human being aided another in time of need. They became intolerant of my arguments and defense that they decided to leave. I heard them whisper going up the stairs and broke out in ridiculous laughter. They informed me of the family court that was going to take place at a small catering hall in Brooklyn. I felt terrified having to face the men in a censored and unlawful court. Two days later, my father and brothers would take me for judgment. My father warned me to cooperate and respect the order of his older relatives ruling in my case. He informed me on our way to the hall that I would have to do whatever they require me in punishment of what I had done.

CHAPTER FIFTEEN

Traditional Court

I felt like a prisoner in a foreign land with rules I couldn't understand enough to believe in and follow. I humbly sat down next to my father on one side and my two brothers on my other side. There were about twenty old men from the family. I kept my head down as my father requested previously. It seemed to me that I would not be given a fair trial. They were the same people who allowed me to be forced into my marriage in the first place. "You ran away from your husband and into the Israeli army. You traveled with a strange man alone. You wrote a book about both of you. There is no way out of this for you than to return to Palestine and live with your husband. We would have ordered to have you killed, but in this country, we can't afford to get lifetime jail for your hideous moves," said my oldest distant uncle. I felt a sudden rush of adrenaline and wanted to get up and demolish the whole place down. I wanted to scream from their injustice and cruelty. "I would never return to him, even if you threatened to kill me. I'm dead anyway if I did return to him. I begged that man to help me out and he did, just like any normal human being would do." My father silenced me by grabbing my arm with fury. I felt like yelling out and running to the streets for help, but they would love to lock me up in a mental institute and claim me insane. They agreed to allow me to stay until I finished my court case with the gunman. I started to realize that they were the ones who assigned that man to get rid of me. They threatened that if I ever go near Joseph again, I would be sorry. They hinted that they would take him away and allow the same gunman to end Joseph's life. I felt that I would be responsible if anything happened to Joseph. It was time to end it with him. I pleaded that I needed a divorce despite what they ruled and I would refuse being deported. After all, I was an American citizen with rights as any other citizen in that country. They agreed to my divorce if I never have any contact with what they considered a foreigner to my nation. I hated putting Joseph's friendship on the bargaining table, but I had no other choice. "We would monitor your trial in person. We will be there at the court that the Supreme Court had issued for you. Finish your case and go home. If we suspect any relationship with that Israeli man, we would kill him while you watch," said my other uncle. I felt my cheeks explode from the burning of their speech. My heart filled with endless tears and sorrow. How could I possibly get rid of the only person who ever cared for me unconditionally? I didn't care where he came from or who he was. They would not understand how I felt. Their minds were locked and someone had lost the key about a hundred years ago. I felt owned by all those relatives. They said that I could have the choice of marrying anyone from their children. Why would I want to repeat the same mistake? I told them. They were stirred in anger. They said that they recognized me as a pretty woman whom they needed to keep a look out for from other men. Not much comfort in that meeting, I wanted to just go home and think of a plan or an idea to help me get through. As we prepared to leave that hall, I looked outside the glass walls and noticed Joseph sitting in his car. I felt the danger of him getting caught. I asked my father for permission to use the ladies' room. He agreed since that gave the other men time to exit the hall. I entered the lavatory in frustration and panic. I instantly pulled out my Iphone. My fingers jittered profoundly, which made it harder for me to dial and call Joseph. I felt excited upon hearing his deep and caring voice. I urged him to disappear before getting sought by anyone from my family. I wondered how he knew where I was. He said our phones came with a tracking device. I thought that was my opportunity to act mad and push him away. "How could you track me and spy on me like that, you don't own me. It's time you went your own way and left me alone."

I hated hurting him and hoped to remain convincingly firm."I thought that you would be in danger, and I needed to make sure that you were fine," he pleaded with a sudden shriek in his voice. "Tell me you didn't mean that, tell me!" I slammed the phone shut in his face. Then I bit the phone hard as my tears fell in abundance. My brother knocked on the restroom's door and demanded that I speed up and get out. I tugged the phone away and proceeded to wash my face consecutively. I felt my father as he stood in wonder at my vigorous scrubbing of my face. I hoped to conceal my heartache and left the bathroom without saying a word to him. I felt my anger transform into an invisible strength. I took stiff steps and walked to my father's car without looking around for Joseph. I couldn't help but hear him press on his gas and noticed him drive away like a wild teenager. Everyone turned to look at the sudden beeping of the cars and the loud screeching coming from the wheels of Joseph's car.

CHAPTER SIXTEEN

Out of Sight

Days passed and I had no contact with Joseph. He sent me text messages, and I would not reply to any. I was fortunate enough to catch him on a televised live interview, which he informed me of in advance. I looked for the writing between his words. Somehow he had become a major celebrity and most talked about man. I looked for his revenge and found it in his statement when he said, "I have been rejected before and plan on finding the right woman for me." He looked straight at the camera. I felt that he could see me through the screen. My heart jumped and I smacked my forehead. I remembered when he stopped me from doing that. I smacked again and again till I cried out loud with the loneliness that occupied me. I wanted to choke him and make him stop torturing me. Being all alone in my family's living room, I felt trapped and not secure. I hated being away from society while everyone else had a life to run about. I surrendered my ears to Joseph's interview and listened with caution. He was asked if he would defend me in the case of the gunman, he replied that if he can get out of it, he would. Again, he smiled straight at the camera. I felt that I had become part of a bigger battle. He seemed to challenge my inner being. I needed to calm down and wait till the end of the interview before attempting to reach him. He flirted with the blond reporter and laughed at every joke he made. I wanted to call the station and submit an anonymous question just to tease him. I wondered how someone can leap from being a best friend to an opponent. I dialed the hotline and waited through the commercial break to be connected to the broadcast. I was introduced as a mystery guest caller and received permission to intervene. "Hello, you're on the air," said the reporter, and Joseph sat up smiling to hear the caller. My voice froze, and I couldn't address him, I couldn't hurt his image. I blamed myself for his new attitude, so I shut the phone line. The fake smile that covered his face was suddenly erased. He became silent and lost his glow. He seemed anxious to escape the interview. He completely changed color and seemed a bit distraught. I thought about calling again, but I resisted. He actually spoke about the political issue in the Middle East. He said that some people dream of making a bridge between the two nations. The reporter interrupted his speech and said, "Isn't that a line from Salwa Adam's book?"

He claimed that it was a general opinion and didn't link it to me. He obviously wanted me to fight him or invent an argument, I thought. He went on talking about the relationship between the Israelis and the Palestinians. He seemed to want to win against both sides. I wondered if he could. The last question from the reporter to Joseph made me want to explode "What is your relationship with Salwa Adam at the moment?" II held my breath in anticipation for a hopeful reply from him.

"Nothing, she's nothing to me and I'm nothing to her," he said as his face turned red. I felt like smashing the TV down, but I feared getting my head smashed by my father. I wanted to scream at him and called him a liar as loud as the house could hold my anguish. He seemed like a good liar, I thought. Why wouldn't he be, his profession helped him obtain tactics that made me seem ignorant. I heard my fathers' car pull over in the driveway. I switched the channels and walked to the kitchen to get a drink of water. I filled the glass with ice cubes first. Nothing could cool the burning inside of me, not even cold water. I sensed extraordinary excitement coming from my parents as they entered the house. I took small sips of the ice water and avoided watching them. They slithered around me and had weird smiles. My father held a mail envelope in his hand. They were horrible at being nice. They asked about my health and if I was feeling better. I knew something had to give. My father asked me to sit down. He said he wanted to discuss something with me. I carried my glass of water along as I took a seat in the living room.

"I want to say that I'm sorry and I hope you could forget everything. Also, you know what I have here: it's an account of your recent earnings from the book you've written. There seems to be six-figure digits in the bank for you!" he said as my mother yelled out of joy. He tried to explain that I made over a million and the numbers keep rising by the hour. He became upset when he noticed that I showed no interest. It didn't take him long before he turned back into his old self. Easily tempered with a hint of violence, he would never change, I thought. He tried to elaborate the number to me. The more he tried, the bigger the number became. He said that he needed money in order to pay his debts and open a new store and more. I had one condition before agreeing to give away any of my new cash pile. I asked for proof of my divorce from Sammy. He hated hearing my request, but I finally could demand it without any fear.

"Why do you want a divorce that fast, do you think you could go back to that Joseph guy?" he snapped.

"No, I don't care about that guy or any other! I want out of Sammy's life first and then you shall have all the money you need."

He said that the divorce process might take long, and he couldn't wait that long. I feared a trap; therefore, my money gave me the strength to blackmail even my father. I felt his invisible hands strangle me, yet he kept seated. I took a long sip from my water. I felt a bit wicked, but he drove me to that. I had to buy and guarantee my own divorce. He immediately jumped to the phone and spoke very loudly to Sammy, asking him to grant me a divorce. In my culture, the man has the power of the divorce. The whole world could convince him, but he had the last say in it. I didn't trust my father at all after what he had put me through. I kept my word and determination stamped. My father worked eagerly with Sammy, and finally, Sammy said he would mail me my divorce papers. I felt happy and free for the first time in years despite the sadness that inhibited my heart. I felt like sharing the good news with a friend of Joseph.

"There is no price for ever considering marrying Joseph. If I think you're seeing him or talking to him, you would see what will happen, not to you, but to him. That way you live with the guilt for the rest of your life, knowing that he died because of your fault," he threatened. He walked away and left me wondering. Who ever said anything about marrying Joseph? That seemed just an overzealous comment. There he went again declaring my future for me and not hearing me out. His words seemed serious and dangerous. My mother seconded the motion of his threat and warned me not to go against my father's authority. She exclaimed that she didn't want me to suffer any more misfortune. I sat staring at the TV and not actually seeing anything on. I went in deep thinking. I felt I owed all my new riches to Joseph. Without him, I could not have gotten that far. I wished I could express my gratefulness to him anyhow. If I sent him a message, he would think that I want to stay in contact and it would be hard to push him away again. If only my parents knew that Joseph was responsible for the new changes that were about to take place in our lives. I knew that in due time the truth would have to come out, but not at that time.

How could I possibly thank him and make sure he remains alive and safe. I owed him that much at least. That the world has created a beast.

I received invitations to speak at talk shows, but I refused. I didn't need the fame, and the fortune made only my family happy. I denied reporter interviews also. Joseph, on the other hand, covered the media. I felt like dying when I saw him surrounded by a crowd of women, begging for his autograph. He had the spotlight all to himself without me to share it with. I did mind him exposing himself to the drooling of those women who didn't even know him or love him. They were attracted to the public figure he represented. I worried that he might get in trouble. He became very popular and outspoken. He tried to reach me a few more times, but I feared answering his messages. He took his hurt to a higher level of public appearances.

CHAPTER SEVENTEEN

Judicial Love

The court day had come and I dressed in expensive yet elegant clothing. I looked forward to catching a real glance at Joseph and then disregarding him. My father walked with me to the court stairs, reporters came charging at us. I smiled and didn't stop for anyone. I headed toward the wide and open stairs of the court building. I felt startled when I noticed Joseph pull over and get out of his car. He stopped for picture taking and some meaningless autographs. I ran ahead of the severe crowd and made it into the building in one piece. I heard those who called my name. I ignored them all. I couldn't believe my eyes when I saw Rachel, Joseph's sister, make her way toward me. My eyes opened wide and my heart was filled with delight. I felt glad that my father had no idea who she might have been. She pulled me over to the side and away from the distraction of the crowd in the lobby. She seemed to target me from the second I entered the building. I instantly gave her a warm hug; she repelled and went right to questioning me. "Look what you've done to my brother, I never saw him like that before. He's killing himself for your attention and you don't even care," she said, standing close to my ear.

"You don't understand that he would be killed if I did give him any attention." And I broke loose from her words. I feared to say anything else or get anyone in trouble. I simply went into the courtroom and took my assigned seat. The courtroom started getting filled with people. I felt shock in my body when I turned to a man calling my name.

"Tom!" I said. He wanted to shake my hand, but my brother held him back.

"Are you okay? How are you?" I asked him compassionately.

"I'm fine, but what the hell have you done to Joseph?" He seemed to think he cared more than I did about Joseph. I felt crushed by the only people I cared about.

The courtroom was filled with everyone except Joseph. He made a grand entrance and avoided me. My heart stopped when he took the seat beside me in court. He had assigned himself as my attorney. He had enough connections to turn anything around. Joseph and I were at a new war, so it came as no surprise how he became my lawyer. My father gave a few fake and loud coughs. He seemed to want to remind me of the threat he made against Joseph. I kept my face aimed at the judge and resisted looking over at Joseph. I only took one look at the gunman sitting by the other table. I felt all eyes on Joseph and I. We were being analyzed by almost everyone. Joseph intoxicated my table with his extremely heavy cologne. That helped keep me from fainting. His smell woke up my senses. He dressed extraordinarily handsome that day. He turned to me and said, "Nothing personal, I'm just doing my job here." His words made me stutter, and I wished for strength to get me through that court session. His words cut my organs like a dagger. He didn't say anything else to me, which made me want to say something. I wrote him on a piece of paper. "I'm sorry and you of all people should understand the dangers I'm in if I continued our friendship."

"Our friendship, what friendship? Is that what you called it?" he yelled out. He seemed to have lost control of himself and didn't care about all the ears that surrounded us. I covered my side of my face with my hand, blocking him from saying anything else. He leaned into my ear and said, "Let's just finish this business here and move on." I wrote a last note. "So why the hell would you represent me?"

That time he wrote back. "Because I needed to end it the right way."

"End it so you can go back to all your adoring fans," I said and couldn't wait to write it down.

"Ah-ha, admit you're jealous and can't stand to see me go to waste," he said as he tucked his tie inside his jacket and pushed back his glasses in pride. He was right in both. Although I felt burnt from jealousy over him, I also feared for his life being wasted at the hands of anyone. The judge apparently watched us writing to each other, and said, "You two are acting like two teens, whenever you're ready to start, Mr. Weisman? Joseph demonstrated great expertise and enthusiasm in the courtroom. He dominated with his eloquence and smooth style. He mocked me in every way possible. He modeled himself in front of me; I turned my head away every time he came near me. I noticed Detective Smith and Detective Harrison in the courtroom as well. Detective Harrison gave me a salute gesture. My case proceeded with ease. The only difficulty was avoiding Joseph. He seemed like he was dancing in that room. Everyone watched him with admiration. I bit my lips a few times in controlling myself from speaking to him. By the time the court session ended, the courtroom felt like burning from the body heat Joseph had sparked. Although we won the case with the gunman serving time in jail, victory remained far from our reach. We were both more upset than before. The time to detach arrived and anxiety took over us. We watched the court officers take the defendant out of the courtroom. Joseph watched my facial expressions. He focused on my head motion, which followed the gunman out. Joseph sat with one hand on his cheek and the other tapping on the wooden table obnoxiously. "One final comment, Counsel Weisman and Ms. Adam, I would like to see both of you in my chambers in fifteen minutes. I'm sure you're familiar where it is located, Counsel Weisman." Joseph sat up straight and alert and replied with eagerness. My father seemed to disagree; he stood up and opposed the idea. He demanded to be present with us. The judge warned my father of possible prison days for lashing out loud in court. No one could argue with the judge's request. I noticed a woman in her late fifties approach Joseph and bent down to his ear level. She rested her head on his shoulders. They spoke in low tones and confidentiality. I had no one to mingle with, so I reviewed the case files to myself. I felt a gentle hand on my shoulder, which surprised me. I looked up and noticed the same woman standing over my head. She introduced herself as Joseph's mother. I immediately stood up and shook her soft hand. She leaned close to me and whispered, "Be careful with my son's emotions. If anything happens to him, you and your whole family would wish you never knew us." I looked at her with astonishment and felt speechless. She had the wrong idea about me, and I had no privacy to speak clearly. I forced a few words without thinking, "Maybe someday you'll understand the sacrifice I had undergone for his sake." Joseph distracted her by standing and cutting in between us. He asked her to take a seat and stop patronizing me. I heard the exhaustion of Joseph's deep breath. He seemed torn and lost his cool. She exclaimed that I'm guilty of torturing him. I didn't know in what sense she pointed out her misconception of me. Her voice became louder as Joseph opened his arms to encompass her angry gestures. I didn't blame her for worrying about her son. She loved him and needed to assert his protection. He asked Rachel to take care of his mother and turned his back to me. Tom ran to help her to her seat and calmed her down. Joseph told her to stay quiet and threatened that the judge might give her some prison time as well. Joseph stroked his hair away from his forehead. He fixed his tie and buttoned his jacket. I heard his chair scratch the floor as he sat. Joseph's mother sat next to a man about her age, I assumed it had to be her husband. He threw his arm around her shoulder to tame her. He showed an older resemblance to Joseph. My disappointment covered my face. That courtroom overflowed with injustice. Rachel came over to Joseph and stood between us. She asked us to go to the judge's order in his chambers. I felt glad to remember, and she couldn't have picked a better time to remind us. My brother rushed to me and warned me against speaking with Joseph. He reminded me of the men waiting to take him down if he transgressed his limits of decency. My brother didn't seem to mind that Joseph might have heard the threats. Rachel slid my chair and asked me to get up and leave with Joseph. As we both stood up, there was sudden complete silence. Only the sound of my high heels echoed in that room. I stomped my way out of that room. I stood a moment outside and waited for Joseph to guide me. He knew where the judge's chamber lay. He broke out of the courtroom. He took giant steps and walked briskly. I stepped into the ladies' room. I went inside and stood by the sink. I waited till the last woman left. She smiled and complimented my suit. I thanked her and watched her exit. I made my hands into fists and punched at the mirrors in front of me. I closed my eyes tight. I held my head down, avoiding the mirror. I didn't want to see the kind of woman I had become. I also blamed myself for the change in Joseph's attitude. I became startled when I picked my head up to look at the mirror. I noticed Joseph's reflection. He stood right behind me. I wondered how I didn't hear him come in. He and I stared at each other through the mirror. I felt like I was caught doing something wrong. I had lost the battle of the "I don't care scheme." He caught me off guard and left me no time to put up a new fake front.

"I know this is difficult for both of us, but how can we teach the world new lessons if we didn't finish learning them?" he said, turning me around. He held my arms with his two hands. I tried to avoid looking in his mesmerizing and passionate eyes because they made me melt. I had to confess the danger he was in and how I had to run as far away from him as possible. He admired my pain and urged me to stay strong.

How could I? Being in front of him ruined all the resistance I tried to fake and build. He said that he didn't care about any threats made toward him. "I only need you and nothing else. I can't imagine living without you."

"I'm sorry, but I can't. Your life is in my hands. Why can't you understand what I'm going through just to keep you alive? I don't want any harm to touch you. I'd rather die first," I said, avoiding looking in his lively green eyes. "There must be a way!," he pulled me closer to his chest. I nearly melted to death before I pushed him away. He attempted to pull me closer. This time I held him tight and would not let go. I lost all my fake resistance.

"We can never survive in this cruel world. I can't live my life worrying about your safety. It's very difficult; you and I," I said in despair.

"But not impossible." He insisted. "I need you, but I need you alive; even if that means keeping away from you forever," I said. I broke away from his embrace. I ran out of the restroom. He chased after me. In the crowded hallways, we tried to appear normal. Joseph kept at my pace. I felt our energy explode as we marched vigorously. Eventually, we reached the judge's chamber. Joseph opened the door and stood along the side, advising me to enter. I brushed through him and squeezed inside. The judge sat on his chair with his back relaxed, and he raised his eyes from underneath his thick eyeglasses. He pointed to the two empty seats by his desk. We sat with our attention focused on him. He chuckled as if he'd just been tickled and took off his glasses. "I have never met a couple as odd as you two." I opened my eyes in doubt. I denied the word he used to refer to Joseph and me as a couple. Joseph

DIVERSE KNOTS

smirked and put one leg over the other. That reminded me of our first time we met in his brother's office. Before we were strangers, but in front of the judge, we were in great danger. My heart dropped, sitting in front of Joseph and a highly respected figure. I listened with anticipation. "I can't have a case in front of me and accept the victim or victims leave my courtroom without a fair hearing," the judge said turning his head from side to side. "We just won the case, Your Honor, so I believe we're not victims," I said because I disliked that word very much. Especially to be given to Joseph. He mentioned that he had reviewed all that had happened to Joseph and I. It seemed that he had taken an interest in our battles. He said that he wanted us to resolve our differences and become everyone's prodigy.

"A violent uprising in your homeland has taken place. Many Israelis and Palestinians were inflicted. The protest started in opposed opinions against the relationship of you two. You may deny it to yourselves, but the rest of the world is sure that you too are mad about each other. It seems to me that you two are inseparable even if you tried.

"Now I don't want to happen to you, like what happened to Romeo and Juliet. You're just as foolish, except you're toiling had gone on longer and caused a real live world stir."

Joseph and I came to a striking yet true realization. We did deny each other in public. I guessed the world noticed what we worked so hard to hide. Joseph's two legs dropped to the floor and his stamina diminished. He looked at me as if for the first time and seemed proud of the judge's findings. I hated being the reason for a riot in my country. It wasn't like those two nations needed a reason to fight. I would never forgive myself for being the cause for their quarrelling. What crime have we committed? Why couldn't a Jewish man help out a Muslim woman without being punished for it? I had suffered long enough and couldn't tolerate any more. Every nation on Earth is allowed to engage freely with one another. The stubbornness of the Arabs and

Jews complicated the peaceful lifestyle needed for survival in that region. No compromising from either side. One agreement leads to a million disagreements. I wished that I could make the two nations get along and live in their own holy hemispheres. I couldn't believe what the judge insinuated. He destroyed all the walls and defenses I lined up against such a confession. He asked us to remain in his office and to come up with a plan that would change the way the world viewed us and fix the situation like two mature adults. He made us seem like two politicians which needed to present a public statement to the world. He left us alone and unattended. I didn't trust myself alone with Joseph. I felt confused and scrambled. I knew we were trapped with our own nets. Things could not have gotten any worse for me then. I felt a great responsibility. I became overwhelmed with the new deal. I couldn't escape Joseph's eyes as he sat there more confident than ever. His silence cut my body and made me shiver. We watched the judge wobble his way out of that room. Once he shut the door from behind him, Joseph crept by my legs and laid his two hands on my lap. He looked up at me and said, "Are we going to chase each other forever or surrender to love?"

"It's impossible to win in a world of misconception. I think we can try and lead them into a new movement," I said, finally having the chance to caress his hair. Tears filled his passionate eyes that made me want to cry as well. My thighs shook as they were touched by an angelic being. Who could claim him an enemy? He blushed like a young kid and smiled.

"You have become my hero and the air that I breathe. My mind knows nothing if it didn't apply to you in some way or another." His tears rolled gently down his face and I wiped them with my hands."Here it goes, I'm crazy in love with you, and so what do you have to say to that?" he said, kneeling on the floor with both knees. "Marry me?" He jerked and nearly fell backward. I laughed at his reaction and reached to bring him back to his old position. He retrieved with excitement and cried heavily. He said yes once, twice, thrice, and kept going till I stopped him. He said, "there is nothing more on earth I want than to marry you, and I love to take you on your proposal. His only regret and concern was that he wished he could run out and buy me a giant diamond ring. I didn't care for anything at that moment, besides Joseph. "Let's get married right here, right now, and whatever happens, let it happen. The ring would have to wait. I'll get the judge to give us our vows. We'll leave this place with a marriage certificate and publish it on the news instantly. There are reporters outside waiting for a scoop, and something like this would be dealt with without hesitation." Joseph jumped with the idea. Although it did sound crazy and out of line, I couldn't withdraw from the deal. Seeing how happy we both transferred, we couldn't answer to anyone. In my Islamic knowledge and past studies, a woman did not require the consent of her family when she remarried. Joseph didn't want to bother with getting anyone's blessings either. It made sense to get a marriage contract and face the consequences as they came. Joseph ran out to get the judge and wasted no time; it felt like a fairy tale, yet we couldn't predict the future. Joseph came back with the judge and a few other colleagues who were also lawyers. Joseph's smile revealed all of his teeth. His tears had disappeared. He called Rachel and Tom to the chambers as well. They came rushing in. The judge seemed impressed and said, "I have to hand it to you. That it is the greatest plan you could have achieved. I have to report it to a higher authority with your permission." Joseph insisted after the contract was signed and legalized. After the elopement, Joseph and I held each others' jittering hands. We faced each other with great anticipation. We stood brave as no two lovers ever did. We reached for our first and not so forbidden kiss. We must have taken a dive into heaven and returned to earth once the kiss had ended. Who knew long it lasted? I threw my arms around Joseph's neck, and buried my face on his shoulder. In his embrace I found my phenomenal shelter. We became one, and no one could deny us anymore. We let go of each other, due to the heavy distractions in the room, Joseph received pats on his shoulders and back from his colleagues. They made their way to me and shook my hand. The room was filled with energy and excitement. Rachel rushed in and hugged Joseph and I at once. Tom seemed excited and a little worried. Joseph put his arm around Tom and said and informed me that Tom had been his friend since childhood. They were more than friends, judging from the constant touching and shoulder patting they exchanged. The judge prepared the documents to be signed. "The American way is the only way these two can get married," he said as he stood between Joseph and I. Rachel stopped us from continuing and asked me if I would accept a ring she had on. Joseph didn't seem to like the idea. He apologized for not having one ready for an extraordinary occasion. He objected to the ring and said that he would buy me one soon. Rachel made it clear that it was no substitute for a real wedding ring. I accepted it as a gift and held it to my lips and kissed it. Joseph took my hand to see how it fit and pressed his lips against my fingers. A rush of immediacy circulated that room. Our hearts pumped louder than thunder. Within moments, Joseph and I were shocked to find ourselves husband and wife. We had the legal proof and witnesses to prove it to the world. A marriage contract for a Jew and a Muslim had never been heard of. We started a revolution and hoped to influence our generation and many more couples from getting involved in wrongdoing. In my religion, any marriage deal is still better than committing the unlawful. Although converting from one religion to another would only leave one side happy. Joseph and I accepted one another despite our commitment to our own religion. Cheers and laughter accompanied our chatting. I wasn't sure where to go after we stepped out of that chamber. The judge asked for copies of the contract and gave it to Tom to deliver it to the press immediately. I hoped that would ease things outside. My family worried about me, but having Joseph near made the worries and pains vanish. Joseph wouldn't let go of my hand. His fingers interlocked mine. He said he admired my proposal and promised to give me a memorable wedding. I didn't think that there was anything more memorable than that day. He said every day would be a day spent in heaven on earth together. The judge received a phone call, and after he finished speaking, he handed it to me. He said that someone important wanted to congratulate me on my bold move. I wondered who it might be. Many figures crossed my mind. The only way I found out was when I spoke to him. I dropped the phone on the floor and screamed. Joseph picked it up instantly. He looked at the judge and asked who is it that made his wife scream like that. I felt embarrassed and out of control when I mentioned that the president of the United States congratulated and praised. "Should I be jealous? We just got married, and you're already cheating on me," he said, and we all laughed. Joseph took the phone and spoke firmly and with respect to the president. It seemed that the president did all the talking because Joseph listened more than he'd spoken. I couldn't stop myself from smiling. I felt my cheeks ache. They were muscles that I rarely exercised. Joseph shut the phone with a satisfied attitude. He raised his chest and stood taller than before. I wondered what he and the president had spoken about. He may have received political advice on how to face the public with our new situation. The news spread like rain on an island. Joseph's father called him and informed him that his mother had collapsed and was unconscious and needed medical attention. Joseph's father said that he waited for the arrival of an ambulance. Joseph's happiness suddenly turned into aggravated consequence. Joseph had to run out and see his mother who waited in the court's lobby. He held my hand and dragged me along. We cut through the crowd and made it into the lobby with exasperation. Joseph said that he didn't trust to leave me behind. "Go with her to the hospital," I advised Joseph. "I can't go and leave you behind, it's far too dangerous for you now," Joseph said. "Don't worry about me, they can't hurt me now. I have new connections." No place felt safer than being with him. We stood by his ailing mother. His father had a frown of disapproval and disappointment. He avoided us and became occupied with aiding his wife. Joseph fell to the floor and tried to speak to his mother. She didn't respond. He asked me to remain with Tom as he took off to the hospital. "I trust Tom to take good care of you while I'm gone."

"I want to come with you instead, and hopefully, I can cut through to your mother and make her accept me."

"No, I'm sorry, I know how she is. She would need more time to get used to the new situation," Joseph said and handed me to Tom. He quickly turned to his mother and left me torn and empty. Joseph struggled to get away from the storming press. They attacked him with harsh questions and unorganized picture taking of him and his family. He jumped inside the ambulance with his mother. I felt horrible by his misfortune and guilt. My father raced toward me along with my brothers. They grabbed me and attempted to walk away. Tom would not allow them. He hid me behind him and was ready to hit anyone who came close. I cried and yelled to stop the fighting. Security came charging as Tom and my father wrestled for a while. Police invaded the scene and ended the fight. With no arrests made, I feared an escalation of troubles to come. I also feared being taken back home by my family members. I didn't regret what I have done. I knew it would hurt for a while, but in the end, it was still my life. Tom persuaded me to come and stay with him until Joseph got back. I knew that my family would consider it unlawful and use it against me. They seemed ruthless and merciless. My father told me that a gunman had followed Joseph and awaited a signal to shoot. Unless I went with him, Joseph was considered dead. I had no other choice; therefore, I urged Tom that Joseph's life was in danger if I didn't leave with my family. He backed up and kicked the chairs in front of him out of frustration. It would be the second time for Tom to let me slip away from his guardianship. We swept through the paparazzi and made it to the car in one piece. I knew my father would not dare kill me, knowing all eyes were on him. He feared prison and had no intentions of going back. In the car, he slapped me hard over and over again until he lost energy. We pulled up by our house. They forced me inside the house. "I'm going to make you regret ever marrying that man. He would never find you," my father said and immediately packed my belongings and told my brother to take me away. I had no idea where I was being driven to. We came close to a deserted area with no sign of residents. The houses stretched far from each other. My brother pulled me into a detached house. It seemed wrecked and needed some exterior repair. It appeared like a haunted house and was ever so unwelcoming. A man with a thick beard opened the door and allowed us in. He seemed familiar with the deal. He instantly helped my brother into the basement and opened another secret door, which seemed like an attic, except it was in the boiler room. I heard my brother call him by the name of Ali. They dumped me there and locked the door behind them. No one would ever find me there, I feared. I wished that I had died and ended all that misery. With no connections to the outside world, I had no hope of being rescued or breaking out. I heard mice chasing each other. I couldn't see them because the little room barely had a light. It must have been a forty-watt lightbulb installed. There were old cartons and old bikes stacked on top of each other. The floor felt concrete and dirty. I felt the dust on my hands. It smelled like an old and rusted tin can. Oil boxes leaked and smeared on the ground. It seemed that I would be spending some time in that new prison. I knew I had people looking for me. I knew Joseph would find me eventually. That had to be the worst jail ever. It seriously felt torturous and creeped me. There went my new and expensive suit. I lost my shoes, and my hair frizzed from fear. I wondered who that man had been. He accepted to take me prisoner without knowing me personally. How could my family trust him of all men? What made him earn that status? I know my father and brothers' jealousy blinded them and anyone around them. There was a small window that couldn't fit a baby through it. I stood up and tried to see an opportunity for running away. It leads to the backyard. I could see some tall trees and overgrown grass from a distance. I screamed when I heard the sound of mice close to my feet. I went back to my spot. I tried to sleep away my fears. I held my knees together and rolled on the floor. I thought to myself. I went from marrying a prince, speaking the president, being a rich woman, to being a pauper, and jailbird. They should've just killed me and got me over with. I couldn't take such harshness anymore. I felt fed up with trying to survive in the jungle of opinionated chiefs. I closed my eyes and thought about the sweetest thing on my mind, Joseph. It seemed I fell asleep until the following day. I always slept longer in depressing situations while others experienced insomnia. I rose and could see the sun's rays enter through the small hole called a window. I noticed the flying dust that the rays defined. I stared at the light ray for a while and wondered if I will ever be given any food or attention. As the sun's rays shifted away by noontime, I heard someone from behind the door. He unlocked the door and made his entrance. It was Ali; he gave me something to eat and gave me no eye contact. I followed him to the door, and he continued disregarding me. He said that what I did had never been done in history. I tried to explain, but he walked out in disappointment. He didn't seem violent or tempered; he was more of a quiet man. No wonder my family trusted him. They knew how to pick out their helpers. My father visited me that day in fury. He kept the door open when he entered; he seemed not too comfortable by setting the conditions. "I won't kill you, I want you to kill yourself," he said. He made it seem like I would help do him a favor, and he wouldn't have to face any form of penalty. He took out a pen and a few pieces of paper; he told me to write a suicide letter. He will return tomorrow and I better have it ready. He also insisted that I leave all my riches in the bank for him only. He sounded excited about the amount. He said that was the only good thing that came out of me. My book was selling faster than rice and bread. Too bad I couldn't enjoy my success or my new marriage. I reminded my father that what I had done was not the end of the world. He said that the attention I was getting drove him crazy, and he couldn't have me that famous and my brothers were not. He envied my new image. It wasn't about wrong or right; it was about jealousy and envy. He said that the world is sympathizing with me and acknowledging me as an important figure. "So why can't you just let me be? You'll see the good that would come out of me. I would open foster and orphanage rescue organizations." I told him I would use my energy and wealth for God's cause and pleasure. He seemed to want it all on a golden platter and not have to share it with anyone. He hated how I may have broken the code that separated the Muslims and the Jews all these years. He said he didn't want the world to follow my trend and what if I did create peace in the Middle East. He said that committing suicide would probably earn me the reputation of trying. I didn't care what my reputation would be if I killed myself. He knew more than I did that suicide was a forbidden Islamic act. He said I earned the right to be killed anyway. He threw the pen and paper in front of me. He headed toward the door, and I said, "What kind of father would do this to his daughter?" He showed no remorse and proceeded to exit. He warned me to have the letter ready and to make sure I included my good-bye to my new husband. He laughed going up those stairs. I called out that I hated him and wished I never knew him. What a wicked and evil plan, and I thought he would actually go through with it. He didn't mention how I would portray killing myself. I refused to write the letter until he agreed to the way I wanted to portray my suicide to the world. He returned the following day and became angry. He gave me a violent push against the walls when he saw that I had the nerve to disobey him. I insisted on one condition that I choose the suicide place and time. He looked at me from a side glance and rubbed his chin while thinking hard and long. He said all he needed was for me to just get out of Earth through death. He said I could choose the place, but he would choose the time. I knew that contract was better than allowing any time. I told him I'll write the letter by tomorrow. I also informed him that I would act like I escaped on my own and throw myself into the ocean. No blood, no pain involved. He agreed to the deal with confidence that there would be no chance for the deal to backfire or blow up. He tormented me by saying that Joseph is covering all news channels pleading to find me. "He actually put up a fairly good sum for anyone who knows anything about you. He offered one-half of a million dollars. He doesn't know that I would keep more than that by killing you." Joseph visited my house two times already. He's the only one sure of my father's intentions to get rid of me. I felt relieved that he left unharmed. My father told me that they had a search warrant for the house. He said that he outsmarted the whole police squad search. I asked my father what if he was being followed? He seemed to have figured it all out entirely. I told him that I would sign over all of my money and future earnings from my book to him. I felt I bargained for my life except he wanted to take both. He said that I caused enough disgrace to his image and that my death remained the only way to regain his honor. He had a mind to confirm his love to me. He said that I've always been his favorite and I didn't appreciate that. He pointed the blame at me for every mentioned incident in the past. He said that he couldn't stand to see the world share with me. "I have the human right to love and be happy, but you're always trying to take that away. It didn't matter if Joseph was Jewish or Muslim to you. You just couldn't let me live any normal life. You allowed the progression of dysfunctional circumstances to accumulate." He yelled and demanded that I shut my mouth. He decided to end the session with a threat. He demanded that I write the suicide letter. He mocked me by saying that I was a writer and it shouldn't be hard to do. He left me tarnished and defeated. I had no choice, but to write my last words on paper. I needed to be careful how to address the situation. Although I wrote the letter for the world, I pictured Joseph reading it only. I wanted to leave him with no regrets and despair. I took time out in silence and weeping before holding tight to my pen. I felt like I held a butcher's knife, and I engaged in ripping my heart out. My main concern remained focused on Joseph's well-being. He deserved a better life than my terrorizing presence.

My father and my two brothers came to me the following morning. I had the letter written and folded in front of me. They entered and picked me up to go upstairs. I went with them without any resistance. They sat me down on a wooden chair. My brother said that he wanted me to record reading my letter on the Internet to assure their innocence. Coming from me, no one would ever suspect that they're involved. I didn't think that they were that smart to come up with such an idea. They told me to fix myself up and sit casually, before they started the recording. I glanced at their friend who watched from a nearby distance. While my father read over the letter, my brothers were getting the camera and computer ready. I called secretly to Ali; he hesitated in approaching me. I informed him of the reward being offered for any information leading to me. He seemed surprised and uninformed. I knew I had a chance when he remained silent and thought for a while. I told him, "Just call 911 and say anything about me quickly please." He retrieved as my father dominated his appearance in front of me. My father was upset about the "I love you to Joseph" part in the letter. I refused to take it off. Before agreeing to read the letter, I needed to know where the crime would take place. My father said I can jump in the ocean at midnight. I felt like dying from just hearing that alone. I shed a few unwanted tears and then I wiped my face. I took a deep breath and prepared for a recording. My brother said I can start. I heard him tell my father the recording button would be on in one second. I sat upward and looked into the camera. I didn't need to read from the paper, I practically memorized it. I wanted to smile and feared laughing when I noticed that they forgot to press the record button, and instead, I was on live. I couldn't believe how ignorant criminals can actually get. I decided to steal some recording time in the hopes of getting traced and found. I asked for a glass of water. I waited till the water arrived. I drank it happily and slowly. I wished to comb my hair, but my brother refused any more delay. The smirk that my old sister knew me for finally showed on my face. I read the letter and changed a few things as I went along. I insisted that I forgave my family for their misunderstanding of me. I noticed that Ali withdrew for a while. I hoped he did what I convinced him to do. He looked like he could use the cash for remodeling his house and his appearance for that matter. I hid my joy of hope and stayed calm as I attended my slightly bruised face in front of the camera. I spoke like a reporter and wasted my time, thanking everyone I ever met. My mood picked up a new and positive attitude. I thought that the authorities had enough time to trace the video of me. I would head out to the ocean by midnight as planned. Unexpectedly, my father yelled, "Stop! This is ridiculous. I can't believe you're making me do this to you." He turned off the web camera and tossed it away to my surprise. There he went off again, blaming me for his actions. He felt disgraced for what has become of him. How could he blame me for his crimes and plotting my own murder? I felt ashamed to be in such a position. My brothers agreed that the whole idea just didn't need to go that way. They sat down and thought among themselves. I wished they would allow me to state my thesis. They outcast me from their conversations. My younger brother said, "Maybe we should just let her go, after all she did get married." My older brother said, "I hate her for what she had done for this family. She ruined all of our reputations."

"I didn't ruin anything, it's you guys who can't think for yourselves without Daddy's command," I interrupted. "One more word from you and I will throw you in the ocean myself," said my father. He seemed frustrated and clueless. They decided to go home and think about what to do with me in the morning. I felt double relieved because the message has been sent out to the world press. They didn't know that I would be found possibly before dawn. I agreed to go back to the basement and hoped to spend my last night in that dreadful room. I heard the heavy stomping their feet as they left. The basement's walls were thin enough for any sound to travel through. I felt a rush of excitement and tranquility. I went from being murdered to reconsideration and a chance to be free. I fell asleep for a good while until I heard loud steps approaching my way. I woke up startled and tried to guess who it might be. My door was unlocked by Ali. He said he wanted to report me and get that sum of money I mentioned earlier as a reward. A man like that needed that money more than my family's friendship. He said, "I helped Joseph because I thought that you really did a heinous Muslim act when you ran away from your husband. Then I read that he abused you and I thought you had every right to. Then you marry that Jewish man against everyone's will, except yours. I realized that you always did the right thing, despite the way it may appear to those around you." He seemed to come to reality and refused to carry any more bad deeds on my behalf. I helped him contact the police; I remembered Detective Harrison's number and told him to dial it for quick response. At 2:30 a.m., I knew Detective Harrison must have been asleep for not answering his phone. I told the man to leave a brief message and include his name and phone number for gaining financial reward. I needed to call Joseph and reassure his mind of my well-being. I called him on Ali's phone. I felt despair and disappointment when he didn't pick up his phone. I thought leaving him a message was just as good.

"Hello, Joseph, this is Salwa, I just wanted you to know that I'm okay and—" The man snatched away the phone from my hands and said, "If you contact them, wouldn't I lose the reward for finding you?"

"I'm sorry, I forgot that. Why don't you call Joseph? He's the one who put up the reward anyway," I said, trying to convince him of cooperating. I thought I just won a world series. It was too late to take back my voice mail to Joseph, which means that the number would easily be traced. The man also spoke to Detective Harrison as well. Things were working out beautifully until I heard my father and brother rush back to us. They heard on the news spread of my live camera recording. My father urged that I needed to leave that house and return home. "You'll go home with us, and if anyone asks you what happened, you say that you changed your mind," my father said, hoping to be free from any accusations or charges. He gave me a look of despise and frowned at me. I refrained from celebrating my survival; it didn't feel like the war had ended. I wondered about the two messages that were delivered to Joseph and Mr. Harrison.

CHAPTER EIGHTEEN

Washed Away!

We left that man's house in the middle of dusk. I felt frightened by the environment and the bad company I had. The wind blew the trees and gave me a chilling effect. I feared walking on the grass at night. Who knew what might have been creeping in that overgrown abandoned garden. We were headed back home when I noticed a police siren from a distance. My brother stepped on the gas pedal and raced home. On our way, we drove by the ocean shore highway. My father looked at the ocean and then back at me. My heart sunk in my feet when he asked my father to stop the car. They wanted an easy way out.

"Since the video has been watched by many, I don't see why we shouldn't continue with our plan. You once were caught trying to jump, so this is the perfect opportunity for all of us," he said to me and looked at my brother for a second approval.

"I would rather you kill me than committing suicide. Maybe in the future when you sit down with yourself, you would suffer in pity and remorse. By then, it will be too late, and you would see how wrong you really were about me," I told them and waited as they made their final decision."Just do it, and get it over with, what good is going to come out of her?" said my older brother.

"All that money you spent from my account, that wasn't good enough. Millions lay at your feet and I willingly donated it to your satisfaction," I said and pushed my brother's chair. Apparently, he couldn't argue any longer; he got out and pulled me out. He grabbed my arm and dragged me to the ocean shore. I cried and screamed out of horror. "Dad, please don't let him do this!" I said, looking back at the same time and running forward. My father came out of the car and followed us hysterically. He was too old and out of shape to keep up.

"Wait! Stop, He said. Why aren't you listening to me?" he yelled, and for the first time, my brother lost his mind and disobeyed.

We crossed through the park and over the benches. My brother waited in front of the ocean gate bars for my father's last words to me. He held my hair in his fist and then I cried more because it reminded me of Sammy's torture and coward tactic.

"Jump in and save us the troubles that come with your name," my brother said, showing me the dark waters ahead. Police sirens were heard nearing our direction. My brother only became tenser and pushed me harder. My father pulled me from my brother's grip. My brother wouldn't let go of my hair. I screamed and tried to break away. My brother regained hold of me and pushed my father away. I knew that my father had created monsters out of his children. He cried out loud to my brother to let me go.

"I'll let her go," said my brother as he dumped me effortlessly into the freezing waters. For the first time in my life, I felt like death. I tasted it in midair, diving into the ocean. I heard the weeping of my brother and father in a last minute plea to retrieve the moment. There was no way of turning back time and all seemed to dive with me into that dark night. I realized that crying served no purpose and drained me out of energy. The sea appeared like a giant beast: it opened its mouth to swallow me. I looked up into the skies for mercy and saving. I noticed flickering lights up above. I fought the beastly ocean from digesting me. My hands pedalled around me. I drank more water than I had in a week. I couldn't fight the thick waters and decided to just let things be. I closed my eyes and made a last prayer to God. I saw a mirage of what I wanted to make my life if given the opportunity. I saw myself as I made a speech at the United Nations. I concluded with a major applause from the international figures present. I felt the reward of making Israelis and Palestinians friends. I saw them in a shared land, streets, and the markets. They lived like the way they lived in New York, door to door, with safety and contentment in their hearts. There mirrored a celebration, my family and Joseph's family as they sat on one table and shared a special feast. With everyone present, they laughed and danced together. I saw white birds that flew with pigeons through the sunny parks and the flowers, they sang in harmony. I saw myself wearing a beautiful white dress with my hair flying loosely all around Joseph. I could hear his laughter and smell his essence. His children ran around in the background. I felt the sun on my cheeks radiating as it brightened the day.

"Salwa, Salwa, no!" Joseph's voice was the last thing I heard. I heard a loud splash and a sudden tight embrace. I felt lifted upward. I kept my eyes closed, yet stood well aware of my surroundings. I threw my head on a helpful shoulder and felt the wind brush away the cold water off me. I could hear everyone, yet that silence stoned my frozen body. Joseph rescued me from the deadly sea; that time I had no intentions to return to life. I wanted to die, for good. I couldn't understand why and how I heard and felt my environment. A helicopter launched Joseph and me out of the sea and onto dry land. Joseph and my father wept like the way a widow would. My brother threw himself on my chest and shook the life out of me. I remained motionless and defenseless.

"Salwa, I'm sorry," he yelled loudly and shook me hard. Joseph snatched him by his shirt and threw him far away. My brother surprisingly didn't return to me and allowed Joseph to take over. Detective Harrison dressed in his pajamas and a big maroon robe asked, "When are you two going to settle this, once and for all? Look what became of the woman whose only crime was that she stepped out of the ordinary and conquered the extraordinary." He reached for my forehead and wiped my wet hair away from my eyes.

"Salwa, if you go, I'll go!" Joseph wept harder. He refused my entrance into the ambulance, and my father broke his grip and took him under his arm. I felt that my death would make them realize how wrong they were and hopefully teach them a lesson. Even though it felt too late, it felt good. I noticed the paparazzi flickering my body for national exposure and entertainment. I remained detached from the worldly drama and hoped to flee as soon as possible. Mercy on earth drained and became less available as long as I lived in it, I thought. My body felt like an inflated water sac, and I felt hands thrust my diaphragm like an old-fashioned fountain pump. Joseph wrestled his way into the ambulance and would not let go. He saddened me and made death harder than it already felt. "You can't go now, everything will be alright, and I promise you, just come back to me. You would never have to shed a tear," he said as he shed tears. "With only a few exceptions, you are well respected and accepted by all. Please don't leave me alone."

I wanted to tell him that I was sorry, but I really wanted all trouble to end for him and myself. The world was not prepared for what we were destined to be. We collided and formed a crazy knot. I had to be the sacrifice, and he had to be the one left behind and become part of a historical moment. Being wed to a Muslim woman earned him enough heartache. I drifted away in his embrace and slowly felt the necessary means to stay alive. I felt his spirit go inside my body, cleaning it out of all ailments. I tasted true love for the first time in my life. Nothing could compare to the sweetness and tenderness. Every love story has one thing in common and that was mutual and unconditional fondness that only experience can best define. Joseph's spirit shined inside of me and gave me a unique revival and immediate strength. I felt his heart beating the life into mine.

CHAPTER NINETEEN

Knot Twist!

"Salwa, Salwa!" I heard Joseph's voice again. I opened my eyes and looked for heavenly beings. Death didn't feel any different than being alive, I thought. A strong light shone onto my face, and I couldn't tell who was behind that light. A sudden commotion of a crowd became visible to my sight. I felt a strong and long embrace by one of the surrounding figures. He squeezed me back to reality. I blinked a few times and looked around me for answers. I noticed an angel resembling Joseph. I felt happy to see such a familiar face. Then I noticed more familiar faces and began to realize that I wasn't in heaven. Most importantly, I hadn't died. I realized I was not in a hospital room or my own room. The curtains on the windows hung majestically. They had more fabric than five blankets put together. A very unfamiliar setting, yet the coziness made me feel like I knew the place before, maybe in another lifetime. The big over fluffed pillows that supported my back felt like giant marshmallows. I felt lost on a large and elevated bed. I felt lost and drowned in the white flowery bed covers. The dresser had a large and gold-framed mirror. Unlike all the mirrors I had seen myself into before. A humongous bouquet of colored flowers stood by the side of the bed on an elegant glass table. I transferred from traumatized to shock when I heard Joseph say, "You're home now! Our home."

My father, mother, and Joseph stood by one side. I looked at Joseph's worn-out face and could see his parents behind him. Rachel and Tom stood at the corner for lack of a closer spot to stand. With Joseph dominating the main dish, no one approached for fear of rejection. "Welcome back, my love," Joseph said warmly. He hopped right by my side. He guarded me from the rest. I smiled, because it was nice to see the two families together in one room and not fighting. "I didn't die?" I asked Joseph. His tears ran down his face and he gave laughter of relief. "No, you have a lot of unfinished business on earth. I need you here, and we all owe you an apology," he said, sniffing his tears away. Joseph's mother and father stood over his shoulders and looked at me with sympathy. She leaned down, kissed my head, and said, "I'm sorry and please accept my apology."

"How are you? How are you feeling? I'm so glad to see you healthy and here," I said as I attempted to reach out to give her a hug. She appeared content and well. She seemed dressed for a special occasion. She wore a two-piece outfit. Pink with a matching skirt. She had on a sweet fragrance that made up for her previous harsh attitude. "This is the wise man himself, my father, John Weisman," Joseph introduced his father proudly. He seemed more of a lenient man than David, the General.

"The things you put us and Joseph through changed us, and our life would not be the same without you in it," he said as he held my hand in a long handshake. Back in Israel, the people were stunned with your marriage to Joseph. I do believe it is the best thing you two could ever have done. You two are the new prodigy for the future generations." I sat up straight. I felt fine and full of energy and life. Despite the traumatic dive, I felt a recovery with each minute. I guessed that it was happiness that healed all wounds, not time as they say. The ocean washed away all my worries and sadness. My parents approached, shyly and remorseful. I never had seen them that humble and pitiful.

My brother called out, "Please forgive me, or if you don't, I'll throw myself from the ocean to get rid of the pain I felt from what I did to my baby sister."

I felt slightly traumatized to look him in the face, so I nodded my head. It would take me a little more time to forget what he had done to me. All I could give in efforts were a nod with closed eyes. He accepted it and ran out of the room. His guilt carried him out. With him, I needed time to heal what he had done. My mother approached and gave me a soft and hug. Joseph had to break her away because she started to make me cry as well. It took me a big jump in the ocean to mend her rigid heart toward me. Tom stepped closer and put his hand on Joseph's shoulder. "You two have driven me out of my mind, now be together and drive each other crazy. No more body guarding for you, and I hope you don't need it anymore."

Rachel stood by Tom's side and said, "We'll leave you alone, that's the best thing we can do for you."

I smiled and took a deep breath. I closed my eyes for a second and felt a tender kiss on my forehead. I opened my eyes and noticed Joseph's harsh chin. He apparently hasn't shaved since the last time I saw him.

"I feel like I sank in a new and bigger ocean, love," I said. With everyone huddled around Joseph and I, Joseph pulled out a small gift box. He handed it to me and then dropped to the floor on his knees. "Let me be the one to ask you this time, for God's sake, will you be mine forever?"

"That depends on how long is forever."

"Just say yes," the crowd said. "I don't need to say yes because I never said no," I said as Joseph continued to insist, "Say yes and make me proud."

"Yes indeed, and there's nothing I want from this moment on than to live for you. I need you to get back on your feet quickly because we have a wedding to attend to," Joseph announced. "Where would you like to get married? A unique and odd couple such as us deserves an exceptional reception place. A place like no other which no one ever had the privilege of doing so," Joseph said as he opened his eyes wide and looked around. "Where and what are you saying? You seem to know, don't tell me, our country!" I said in fear.

"You, my darling, and I are going to have our wedding at the White House!" he said. "Remember when I spoke with the president in the judge's office, he invited us to his White House to show the world the way it ought to be done." We all laughed. I couldn't believe my ears, and my heart was filled with inspiration from the news. Joseph said that he couldn't keep it a surprise. He hoped the president would understand his need to deliver a happy and extraordinary pump into my heart. The world is looking forward to such an event. Joseph watched patiently as everyone gave me a kiss and said their farewells. They each had a chance to say a few kind and exceptional words. Joseph waved eagerly in saying good-bye to everyone. He instantly shut the door behind them and turned around and looked at me. As if they didn't just exist, he faced me with relief. For the first time, I didn't run away and planned to always be there with him. He stood behind the door and stared at me from a distance. I stared back with an irresistible smile. "Well, well, what do you have to say to me, Mrs. Weisman? Did you really think you can just die and leave me to suffer?" he said as he roamed around slowly.

"What do you have to offer in compensation for almost leaving me behind? What can you give me in return?"

"I give you my heart and what's left of my mind," I said as he took a big dive next to me. We screamed from laughter at his sudden stunt as he bounced off the bed and dropped on the floor. I held out my hand to help pick him up. He jumped back up and attempted again; with great success, he landed in my arms. Joseph lay beside me. He held my hand and interlocked our fingers together. We proudly looked at the diamond ring as it represented the most beautiful and meaningful stone in history. Gazing into his endless soul, I felt like I conquered the world.

www.ingramcontent.com/pod-product-compliance
Lightning Source LLC
LaVergne TN
LVHW091553060526
838200LV00036B/818